STARRY FLAG
SERIES
OLIVER OPTIC

Down the River; or, Buck Bradford and His Tyrants

Oliver Optic

DOWN THE RIVER;

OR,

BUCK BRADFORD AND HIS TYRANTS.

BY

OLIVER OPTIC,

AUTHOR OF "YOUNG AMERICA ABROAD," "THE ARMY AND NAVY STORIES," "THE WOODVILLE STORIES," "THE BOAT-CLUB STORIES," "THE RIVERDALE STORIES," ETC.

1896.

THE SETTLEMENT

TO

MY YOUNG FRIEND

WILLIAM H. LOW

This Book

IS AFFECTIONATELY DEDICATED.

PREFACE

"DOWN THE RIVER" is the sixth of the continued stories published in "OUR BOYS AND GIRLS," and the last of "THE STARRY FLAG SERIES." It is the personal narrative of Buck Bradford, who, with his deformed sister, made an eventful voyage down the Wisconsin and Mississippi Rivers, to New Orleans. The writer's first book—not a juvenile, and long since out of print—was planned during a long and tedious passage up the Father of Waters; and it seems like going back to an old friend to voyage again, even in imagination, upon its turbid tide.

Buck Bradford tells his story to suit himself; and the author hopes it will also suit the young reader. Whatever moral it may contain will be found in the reading; and the writer trusts it will impart a lesson of self-reliance, honesty, and truth, and do something towards convincing the young reader that it is best always to do right, whatever the consequences may be, leaving results, in the choice between good and evil, to take care of themselves.

However often the author may be called upon to thank the juvenile public for the generous favor bestowed upon his books, he feels that the agreeable duty cannot be so frequently repeated as ever to become a mere formality; for with each additional volume he finds his sense of obligation to them for their kindness renewed and deepened.

WILLIAM T. ADAMS.

HARRISON SQUARE, MASS.,

October 28, 1868.

CONTENTS.

CHAPTER I.
Two of the Tyrants

CHAPTER II.
Flora Bradford

CHAPTER III.
On the Defensive

CHAPTER IV.
Who is Master

CHAPTER V.
A Battle at Long Range

CHAPTER VI.
Squire Fishley

CHAPTER VII.
After Midnight

CHAPTER VIII.
Miss Larrabee's Letter

CHAPTER IX.
The Hungry Runaway

CHAPTER X.
What Sim Gwynn Wanted to see me for

CHAPTER XI.
Building the Raft

CHAPTER XII.
SQUIRE FISHLEY MAKES IT RIGHT

CHAPTER XIII.
NEAR UNTO DEATH

CHAPTER XIV.
WHO ROBBED THE MAIL

CHAPTER XV.
THE DEPARTURE

CHAPTER XVI.
DOWN THE RIVER

CHAPTER XVII.
NIGHT ON THE RIVER

CHAPTER XVIII.
AT THE MOUTH OF THE OHIO

CHAPTER XIX.
AFTER THE EXPLOSION

CHAPTER XX.
EMILY GOODRIDGE

CHAPTER XXI.
FLORA AND HER PATIENT

CHAPTER XXII.
THE END of the VOYAGE

CHAPTER XXIII.
CLARENCE BRADFORD

CHAPTER XXIV.
UP THE RIVER

CHAPTER XXV.
Two Hours in Jail

CHAPTER XXVI.
Conclusion

CHAPTER I.

TWO OF THE TYRANTS.

"HERE, Buck Bradford, black my boots, and be quick about it."

That was what Ham Fishley said to me.

"Black them yourself!"

That was what I said to Ham Fishley.

Neither of us was gentlemanly, nor even civil. I shall not apologize for myself, and certainly not for Ham, though he inherited his mean, tyrannical disposition from both his father and his mother. If he had civilly asked me to black his boots, I would have done it. If he had just told me that he was going to a party, that he was a little late, and asked me if I would assist him, I would have jumped over his head to oblige him, though he was three inches taller than I was. I am willing to go a step farther. If this had been the first, or even the twentieth, time that Ham had treated me in this shabby manner, I would have submitted. For three years he had been going on from bad to worse, till he seemed to regard me not only as a dog, but as the meanest sort of a dog, whom he could kick and cuff at pleasure.

I had stood this sort of thing till I could not stand it any longer. I had lain awake nights thinking of the treatment bestowed upon me by Captain Fishley and his wife, and especially by their son Ham; and I had come deliberately to the conclusion that something must be done. I was not a hired servant, in the ordinary sense of the term; but, whether I was or was not a servant, I was entitled to some consideration.

"What's that you say?" demanded Ham, leaping over the counter of the store.

I walked leisurely out of the shop, and directed my steps towards the barn; but I had not accomplished half the distance before my tyrant overtook me. Not being willing to take the fire in the rear, I halted, wheeled about, and drew up in order of battle. I had made up my mind to keep perfectly cool, whatever came; and when one makes up his mind to be cool, it is not half so hard to succeed as some people seem to think.

"I told you to black my boots," said Ham, angrily.

"I know you did."

"Well, Buck Bradford, you'll do it!"

"Well, Ham Fishley, I won't do it!"

"Won't you?"

"No!"

"Then I'll make you."

"Go on."

He stepped up to me; but I didn't budge an inch. I braced up every fibre of my frame in readiness for the shock of battle; but there was no shock of battle about it.

"I guess I'll let the old man settle this," said Ham, after a glance at me, which seemed very unsatisfactory.

"All right," I replied.

My tyrant turned on his heel, and hastened back to the store. Ham Fishley's father was "the old man," and I knew that it would not be for the want of any good will on his part, if the case was not settled by him. I had rebelled, and I must take my chances. I went to the barn, harnessed the black horse to the wagon, and hitched him at a post in the yard, in readiness to go down to Riverport for the mail, which I used to do every evening after supper.

Of course my thoughts were mainly fixed upon the settlement with the old man; and I expected every moment to see him rushing upon me, like an untamed tiger, to wreak his vengeance upon my head. I was rather surprised at his non-appearance, and rather disappointed, too; for I preferred to fight the battle at the barn, or in the yard, instead of in the house or the store. Though my thoughts were not on my work, I busied myself in sweeping out the horse's stall, and making his bed for the night.

"Buck! Buck! Buck!" called Mrs. Fishley, from the back door of the house.

She always called three times; for she was a little, snappy, snarling woman, who never spoke pleasantly to any one, except when she had company, or went to the sewing circle.

"Here, marm!" I replied.

"Come here; I want you!" she added, clear up in the highest tones of her voice, which sounded very much like the savage notes of an angry wasp.

It was some consolation to know, under the peculiar circumstances, that she wanted me, instead of "the old man," her lord and master, and that I was not called to the expected settlement, which, in spite of my fixed determination, I could not help dreading. Mrs. Fishley wanted me—not her husband. She was always wanting me; and somehow I never happened to be in the right place, or to do anything in the right way.

Mrs. Fishley believed she was one of the most amiable, self-denying, self-sacrificing, benevolent women in the world. Nobody else believed it. She had to endure more trials, bear more crosses, undergo more hardships, than any other housekeeper in town. She had to work harder, to think of more things, stagger under more burdens, than all her female neighbors put together. If she ever confessed that she was sometimes just a little cross, she wanted to know who could wonder at it, when she had so much to do, and so many things to think of. Job could be patient, for he had not her family to look after. The saints and martyrs could bow resignedly at the stake in the midst of the flaming fagots; but none of them had to keep house for a husband and three children, and two of them not her own.

To make a fair and just division of Mrs. Fishley's cares, one tenth of them were real, and nine tenths of them were imaginary; and the imaginary ones were more real to her than the actual ones. They soured her temper,—or, more properly, her temper soured them,—and she groaned, complained, snarled, snapped, and fretted, from very early on Sunday morning to very late on Saturday evening. Nothing ever went right with her; nothing ever suited her. If a thing was one way, that was the especial reason why it ought to have been some other way.

She always wanted her own way; and when she had it—which she generally did—it did not suit her any better. I am inclined to think that Captain Fishley himself, at some remote period, long before I was born, had been a more decent man than he was at the time of which I write. If he ever had been, his degeneracy was easily explained; for it would not have been possible for a human being, in daily contact with such a shrewish spitfire as his wife, to exist untainted in the poison which floated in the atmosphere around her.

This was the woman who inflicted herself upon the world, and upon me, though I was by no means the greatest sufferer. If the mischief had stopped here, I could have borne it, and the world could not have helped itself. To me there was something infinitely worse and more intolerable than my own trials—and they were the trials of my poor, dear, deformed, invalid sister. Tender, loving, and patient as she was under them, her sufferings made my blood boil with indignation. If Mrs. Fishley had treated Flora kindly, she would have been an angel in my sight, however much she snapped and snarled, and "drove me from pillar to post." The shrew did not treat her kindly, and as the poor child was almost always in the house, she was constantly exposed to the obliquities of her temper.

My mother, for several years before her death, had been of feeble constitution, and Flora had the "rickets" when she was a babe. She was now twelve years old, but the effects of the disease still lingered in her frame. Her limbs were weak, her breast-bone projected, and she was so drawn up that she looked like a "humpback." But what she lacked in body she more than made up in spirit, in the loveliness of an amiable disposition, in an unselfish devotion to others, in a loving heart, and a quick intelligence. She endured, without complaint, the ill nature of Mrs. Fishley, endeavoring, by every means in her power, to make herself useful in the house, and to lighten the load of cares which bore down so heavily upon her hostess.

Mrs. Fishley called me, and I hastened to attend upon her will and pleasure, in the back room. I knew very well that it would make no difference whether I hurried or not; I should "have to take it" the moment she saw me. If I was in the barn, I ought to have been in the shop; if in the shop, then I should have been in the barn—unless she had company; and then she was all sweetness, all gentleness; then she was all merciful and compassionate.

"What are you doing out there?" snarled she. "I've been out in the street and into the store after you, and you always are just where no one can find you when you are wanted."

I didn't say anything; it wasn't any use.

"Take that bucket of swill out, and give it to the pigs; and next time don't leave it till it is running over full," she continued, in the same amiable, sweet-tempered tones. "It's strange you can't do anything till you are told to do it. Don't you know that swill-pail wants emptying, without being told of it?"

"I always feed the pigs three times a day whether the pail wants emptying or not," I ventured to reply, in defence of the pigs rather than myself.

"There, carry it along, and don't spill it."

The pail was filled even with the brim, and it was simply impossible to avoid spilling it.

"What a careless fellow you are!" screamed she, her notes on the second added line above the treble staff. "You are spilling it all over the floor! I wish you could learn to do anything like folks!"

I wished I could too; but I did not venture to suggest that if she had not filled the pail so full, and even run it over herself before I touched it, I might have carried it "like folks." It was no use; she always got the better of me in an argument. I fed the pigs, as I always did, before I went after the mail, and carried the pail back to the shed. The door of the kitchen was open, and Mrs. Fishley was returning to her work as I entered.

"You careless child! What do you mean by letting those cakes burn?" I heard her cry to poor Flora, who was sitting in her arm-chair by the cooking-stove, whereon Mrs. Fishley was baking flapjacks for supper.

"I didn't know—"

"You didn't know, you careless hussy!" exclaimed Mrs. Fishley, seizing her by the arm, and lifting her roughly out of her chair.

"O, don't!" groaned poor Flora.

I could not stand that. I rushed into the kitchen, seized poor Flora's tyrant by the shoulders, and hurled her half way across the room. My blood was up to the boiling point.

CHAPTER II.

FLORA BRADFORD.

I HAD never seen Mrs. Fishley use violence upon my poor sister before, though I afterwards learned that this was not the first time. I was a solid-built, stout fellow of sixteen; and when I seized the shrew by the shoulders, I was in real earnest. I had not made up my mind for this occasion to keep cool, and I did not keep so. I was as mad as a bear robbed of her cubs.

The idea of Mrs. Fishley's taking my poor deformed sister by the arm, and shaking her, was too revolting, and even horrible, to be endured. If I could bear everything else, I could not bear that. At the present time, I have this pleasant consciousness, that I did not strike the woman; I only grasped her by the shoulders, and hurled her away from her victim. It was a vigorous movement on my part, and Mrs. Fishley staggered till she saved herself by taking hold of a chair. She gathered herself up, and her eyes flashed fire.

"You rascal, you! What do you mean?" gasped she; and at the same instant she rushed towards Flora, who was trembling with terror in her chair.

"Stop a minute, Mrs. Fishley," I added.

"You rascal, you!" repeated she, looking first at me, and then at Flora.

"If you put the weight of your little finger on my sister again, I'll tear you in pieces," I continued, with both fists clinched.

"What do you mean, you serpent, you?"

"You touch her again, and you will know what I mean."

"Don't, Buckland, don't," pleaded poor Flora, alarmed by the hostile demonstration before her.

"I should like to know!" cried Mrs. Fishley.

As she did not tell me what she should like to know, I did not tell her. I stood upon the defensive between the virago and my sister's chair.

SHE RUSHED TOWARDS FLORA.

"Did any one ever see such a boy!" continued the termagant, her tones a whole octave above the treble staff, as it seemed to me. "How dare you put your hand on me?"

"I dare."

"You rascal, you!"

"You may snap and snarl at me as much as you like; I don't mind it; but you shall not abuse my sister."

"Abuse your sister, you wretch!" said she, the words hissing from her mouth. "I should like to know!"

"You will know if you touch Flora again," I answered.

Somehow I felt as though Mrs. Fishley was not getting the better of me in this argument; and I soon came to the conclusion that she thought so herself, for she settled into a chair, and began to exhibit some symptoms of hysterics.

"O, dear me!" she groaned. "I don't have to work enough to kill common folks, I don't have more trials than any living being, but something new must come upon me. There, I shall give up!"

"You must give up abusing Flora," I put in.

"How dare you tell me I abuse her?" snapped she. "Haven't I taken the best of care of her? Haven't I made her clothes for her? Haven't I nursed her when she was sick? Haven't I done for her ever since she came into the house?"

I don't think she had the least idea that she was not the best friend Flora had in the world, so blind are many people to their own errors and shortcomings.

"She has had enough to eat, and enough to wear; and my brother has paid for all she has had," I added. "But you are continually scolding at her, browbeating her, and making her as uncomfortable and unhappy as you can."

"Scolding her!" almost whistled Mrs. Fishley, so high was the key. "I never scold at any one. I never was a scolding woman."

"Gracious!" I exclaimed, mentally.

"When things don't suit me, I'm apt to say so; but I never scold," whined the shrew. "Whatever people may say of me, they can't call me a scolding woman."

Was it possible she thought so!

"I don't want to make any trouble, Mrs. Fishley," I replied, when she paused, rather for want of breath than for any other reason.

"Mercy! I shouldn't think you did! Ain't you ashamed of yourself to treat me as you did? You push me about as though you thought I wasn't anybody."

"Are you not ashamed of yourself for shaking that sick child?" I retorted.

"I didn't shake her."

"Then I didn't push you."

"You are getting to be a very bad boy, Buck Bradford; and you haven't heard the last of this," she said, rising from her chair, and restoring the griddle to the stove, which Flora had taken off. "I should like to know! Can't I speak to that girl without being treated in that manner? She would let the cakes all burn up before she would touch them."

"I didn't know they were burning, Mrs. Fishley," pleaded Flora. "You didn't tell me to see to them."

"Suppose I didn't tell you! Didn't you know enough not to let them burn? You are a careless, indifferent girl, and it don't make no difference to you how much trouble you make for a body."

"I would have seen to the cakes, if you had spoken to me."

"I don't care anything about the cakes, anyhow," I interposed. "If you can't help scolding Flora, you must keep your hands off her."

"You don't care anything about the cakes! I should like to know! Well, we'll see about it! I'll know who rules here, I vum! I'll call Mr. Fishley! We'll see if you don't care!" rattled Mrs. Fishley, as she bolted from the kitchen through the entry into the store.

"O, Buckland, what will become of us!" exclaimed Flora, rising with difficulty from her chair, and throwing herself upon my breast.

"Don't be afraid, Flora," I replied, pressing her to my heart, while the tears started in my eyes. "She shall not abuse you, whatever happens to me. While she did it only with her tongue, I bore it; but when she took hold of you, I couldn't stand that, Flora—no, I could not."

"I can bear it very well, Buckland." She never called me "Buck," as everybody else did about the place. "I only fear what they will do to you."

"I can take care of myself, dearest Flora. I am strong and tough, and I can stand almost anything," I answered, pressing her to my heart again, for she seemed to be the only person in the world who loved me.

And how I loved her—poor orphan child, weak, sick, and deformed! It seemed to me it would have been different if she had been well and strong, and able to fight her own battle with the hard and cruel world. She was helpless and dependent, and that which shut her out from the rest of the world endeared her to me, and wound her in with every fibre and tendril of my heart.

Mrs. Fishley did not immediately return; neither did her husband appear upon the battle-field; and I concluded that she could not find him.

While, folded in each other's arms, we waited in almost breathless anxiety for the coming of our tyrants, let me give the reader a few necessary particulars in regard to our antecedents and surroundings.

Torrentville, where the story opens, is situated in the south-western part of Wisconsin, though, for obvious reasons, it will not be found on the map. It was located on a stream, which we called the "Creek," though it has since received a more dignified and specific name, about seven miles from Riverport, on the Wisconsin River. At the time of which I write it contained two thousand inhabitants. Captain Fishley—he had been an officer in the militia in some eastern state, and his title had gone west with him—kept the principal store in the place, and was the postmaster.

My father had moved from the State of New York to Torrentville when I was eight years old, and soon after the death of my mother. He had three children, Clarence, Flora, and myself. He bought a farm just out of the village, employed a housekeeper, and for four years got along very well. But he was too ambitious, and worked too hard for his constitution. After a four years' residence in the west, he died. That was a sad day to us, for he was the kindest of fathers. Poor Flora scarcely ceased to weep, at times, for a year, over the loss of her only parent.

Captain Fishley was appointed administrator of the estate, and when it was settled there was hardly fifteen hundred dollars left. My brother Clarence was just twenty-one when my father died, and he was appointed the guardian of Flora and myself. He was considered a very smart young man, and no one doubted his ability to take care of us. But he was dissatisfied with Torrentville; there was not room enough for a young man of his ability to expand himself. He had no taste for farming, and for two years had been a clerk in Captain Fishley's store. He wanted to go to New Orleans, where he believed he could make his fortune. About a year after the death of his father, he decided to try his luck in the metropolis of the south-west.

Clarence was a good brother, and I am sure he would not have gone, if he had not felt satisfied that Flora and myself were well provided for. I was then a boy of thirteen, handy at almost anything about the farm, the house, and the garden, and Captain Fishley wanted me to come and live with him. Clarence agreed to pay Flora's board, so that she was a boarder at the house of the Fishleys. It was stipulated that I should go to school, and do certain "chores" for my board, while Clarence paid for my clothes. My principal work, and all that the captain said I should be required to do, was to take care of the horse, and go after the mail every evening.

Instead of this, I was compelled to be at the beck and call of all upon the place, including Ham, the captain's only son, and miserably spoiled at that. Before I had been a year in my new home, I was dissatisfied, for the cloven heels of the three members of the family had appeared. I was crowded with work, picked upon, insulted, and trodden under foot. Perhaps I could have endured my fate, if poor Flora, upon whom our tyrants had no claims, had fared well.

We heard from Clarence occasionally, and learned in general terms, from his letters, that he was doing very well. I did not like to bother him with complaints, and I did not do so till existence had become almost a burden. I think Clarence wrote back to the captain, and for a time there was some improvement in our condition; but it soon became worse than before. I repeated my complaint. My brother wished us to get along as well as we could till he could spare the time to visit us; but that time had not yet arrived.

A few days before my story opens, early in April, I had a letter from him, saying that he was well established in business for himself, and that he would certainly come to Torrentville in October, as soon as the sickly season was over, and take us to New Orleans. He added that he should be married before that time, and would bring his wife with him. This was joyful news, but it was a dreary while to wait.

The door suddenly opened, and Mrs. Fishley bounced into the kitchen, followed by her husband, both of them apparently wrought up to the highest pitch of anger by my misdeeds.

CHAPTER III.

ON THE DEFENSIVE.

AT the approach of Captain Fishley, I felt the shudder that swept through the feeble frame of Flora, as she stood infolded in my arms. I gently placed her in the chair again, and released myself from her clinging embrace; for I realized that, in the brief moment left to me, it was necessary to prepare for war. I knew the temper of Captain Fishley; and, though he had never yet struck me, I believed that it was only because I had been all submission.

I was fully resolved to defend myself, and especially to defend Flora. I picked up the heavy iron poker which lay on the back of the stove, and placed myself in front of my trembling sister. The captain was a brute, and his wife was hardly better than a brute. I feared that she, supported by her husband, would again lay violent hands upon Flora, knowing that such a course would sting me deeper than a blow upon my own head.

I did not flourish the poker, or make any irritating demonstrations with it; on the contrary, I held it behind me, rather for use in an emergency than to provoke my tyrants. I was not disposed to make the affair any worse than the circumstances required, and by this time I was cool and self-possessed. Perhaps my critical reader may wonder that a boy of my age should have set so high a value upon controlling his temper, and preserving the use of his faculties in the time of peril, for it is not exactly natural for boys to do so. Youth is hot-blooded, and age and experience are generally required to cool the impetuous current that courses through its veins.

My father—blessings on his memory—had taught me the lesson. One day, a fire in the long grass of the prairie threatened the destruction of all our buildings. Clarence and myself went into a flurry, and did a great many stupid things, so excited that we did not know what we were about. Father stopped in the midst of the danger to reprove us, and gave us such a solemn and impressive lesson on the necessity of keeping cool, that I never forgot it. Then he told us to harness the horses to the plough. Clarence struck a furrow along the imperilled side of the house; my father mowed a wide swath through the tall grass, and I raked it away. Before the fire reached us, we had made a barrier which it could not pass. We kept cool, and fought the devouring element with entire success.

I do not mean to say that I never got mad; only that, when I had a fair chance to think an instant, I nerved myself to a degree of self-possession which enabled me to avoid doing stupid things. Such was my frame of mind on the present occasion, and I coolly awaited the coming of the tyrants. Both of them were boiling over with wrath when they entered the kitchen, and rushed towards me so fiercely that I thought they intended to overwhelm me at a single blow.

"What does all this mean, Buck? What have you been doing?" demanded Captain Fishley, as soon as he had crossed the threshold of the room.

I deemed it advisable to make no answer.

"I'll teach you to insult your betters!" he continued, as he rushed forward, with arms extended, ready to wreak his vengeance upon me.

I was satisfied that the blow was to come with the word, and I slung the poker over my shoulder, in the attitude of defence.

"Hold on, Captain Fishley!" I replied.

He had evidently not expected any such demonstration. He had no occasion to suspect it, for previously I had been uniformly submissive, not only to him and his wife, but even to Ham, which had always been a much harder task. The tyrants halted, and gazed at me with a look of stupefied astonishment.

"What are you going to do with that poker?" asked the captain, after a long breath, in which much of his wrath seemed to have evaporated.

"Defend myself," I replied.

"Do you mean to strike me with that poker?"

"Not unless you put your hands on me or my sister. If you touch me, I'll knock you down, if I have to be hanged for it," was my answer, deliberately but earnestly uttered.

"Has it come to this?" groaned he, completely nonplussed by the vigorous show of resistance I made.

"Yes, sir."

"I think it is time something was done," he added, glancing around the room, apparently in search of some weapon.

"I think so too, and I am going to do something, if need be."

"What are you going to do?"

"If you want to talk, I'll talk. I wish you to understand that I'm just as cool as well-water, and this thing has gone just as far as it's going to."

"What do you mean by that, you scoundrel? What thing?"

"My sister Flora is a poor, weak, sick child. She isn't your servant, nor your wife's servant; and she shall not be kicked round by either one of you. That's all I have to say."

"Who has kicked her round?" growled the captain.

"Mrs. Fishley has done just the same as to kick her. She took her by the arm, dragged her out of her chair, and was shaking her when I stepped in."

I was particular to state the facts thus explicitly, because I did not believe Mrs. Fishley had been careful to include this portion of the affair in her complaint to her husband.

"It's no such thing! I should like to know!" exclaimed Mrs. Fishley, who, by some miracle, had been enabled to hold her tongue thus far.

"I saw her do it," I added.

"It's no such thing!"

"Didn't you take her by the arm?" I demanded.

"Well, I did just touch her on the arm, but I didn't hurt her none. I wouldn't hurt her for a million dollars."

"Let Flora speak for herself," I continued. "What did she do to you, Flora?"

"I don't like to say anything about it, Buckland. She didn't hurt me much," answered the terrified child.

"You see, she won't say I shook her, or did any such awful thing," said the virago, triumphantly.

"Speak, my dearest sister. We had better settle this matter now," I added.

"She did take me by the arm, pull me out of the chair, and was shaking me, when you interfered," replied the poor girl, trembling with fear of the consequences of her truthful confession.

"Well, I never!" gasped Mrs. Fishley.

Captain Fishley evidently believed that his wife was lame; but this did not make much difference to him. He was a tyrant and a bully; but, as tyrants and bullies always are, he was a coward, or he would have demolished me before this time. He had a wholesome respect for the poker, which I still kept in readiness for immediate use.

"No matter whether Mrs. Fishley touched the child or not," said he, savagely. "No boy in my house shall insult my wife, or raise his hand against her."

"And no man or woman, in this or any other house, shall raise his hand against my sister," I answered.

"She sat there like a log of wood, and let the flapjacks burn," snarled Mrs. Fishley.

"She hadn't anything to do with the flapjacks. Flora boards here, and isn't anybody's servant," I replied.

"I should like to know! Is that girl to sit there before the fire and let whatever's on the stove burn up before she'll raise her hand to save it?"

"It's no use of talking," said I. "You know all about it as well as I do. All I have to say is, that Flora shall not be abused by anybody, I don't care who it is."

"Nobody's going to abuse her," snapped the shrew.

"I've got another account to settle with you, Buck Bradford," continued Captain Fishley. "Did Ham tell you to black his boots?"

"He did."

"And you told him you wouldn't?"

"I told him so."

"What do you mean, you rascal?"

"I only meant that I wouldn't do it. That's all I meant."

"I should like to know what we're coming to!" ejaculated Mrs. Fishley.

"We are coming to an understanding, I hope," I answered.

"I hope so too, and I mean to do it," added the captain. "High times we're having here, when the boys won't do what they are told, and then take the poker when they're spoken to."

"Captain Fishley, I think there are two sides to this question. The agreement my brother Clarence made with you was, that I should take care of the horse and go after the mail for my board. That's what he said to me in one of his letters. Instead of that, you make me do all the dirty work about the place, and run from pillar to post at everybody's beck and call."

"That's all you're good for," interposed Captain Fishley, sourly.

"Perhaps it is; but that's not what my brother, who is my guardian, agreed to have me do. You have kept me at home from school half the time—"

"Too much learning spoils boys."

"That wasn't what spoiled you. But that's nothing to do with the agreement."

"None of your impudence, you saucy young cub," said he, shaking his head, and moving a step nearer to me; whereat I demonstrated mildly with the poker.

"I don't mean to be impudent, but I won't be treated like a dog any longer. I was willing enough to do all I was told, even if it wasn't according to the agreement; but I get blowed up twenty times a day by all hands. Ham never speaks civilly to me, and treats me like a nigger servant. This thing has gone just as far as it can go. I have made up my mind not to stand it any longer."

"We'll see," replied the captain, grinding his teeth and puckering up his lips.

"But I don't want to fight, or have any trouble, Captain Fishley," I proceeded, more gently, for I had warmed up considerably as I recited the history of my wrongs. "If Ham wants me to black his boots, and will ask me civilly to do so, I will do it, though that's not my work, and my brother never meant that I should be anybody's boot-black."

"You will do what you are told to," bullied the masculine tyrant.

"And not meddle with things in the house," added the feminine tyrant.

"All I ask is, that Flora shall be let alone, and to be used fairly myself," I continued. "I will do the work just as I have done till October, if I can be treated decently. That's all I have to say."

"That isn't all I've got to say," replied the captain. "Buck Bradford, drop that poker!"

"I will not."

"You won't?"

"Not till I think it is safe to do so."

"Do you think I'm going to be threatened with a poker in my own house?"

"I won't threaten you if you'll let me alone. I've said all I have to say."

I know very well that Captain Fishley had not pluck enough to touch me while I had the poker in my hand; and I was fully satisfied that Mrs. Fishley would not meddle with Flora again very soon. The scene was becoming rather embarrassing to me, and I decided either to end it or to shift the battle-field. I turned and walked towards the back room. As one dog pitches into another when the latter appears to show the white feather, Captain Fishley made a spring at me, hoping to take me in the rear. I was too quick for him, and, facing about, I again drew up in the order of battle.

"We'll settle this another time. You haven't seen the end of it yet," said he, as he turned and walked into the store.

CHAPTER IV.

WHO IS MASTER.

I REMAINED in the back room long enough to assure myself that Mrs. Fishley did not intend to put a rude hand upon Flora. I even ventured to hope that she was ashamed of herself, and would not repeat the dastardly act. I went to the barn to consider the situation. I felt just as though I had won the victory over my tyrants in the present battle; but I was confident that the conflict would be renewed at some more favorable time.

Like all small-minded men, like all tyrants and oppressors, Captain Fishley was a revengeful person. He would wait till he caught me napping, and then spring some trap upon me. He would delay his vengeance till some circumstances conspired against me, and then come down upon me with the whole weight of his malignity. I determined to keep a sharp lookout upon all his movements, and especially to avoid all cause of offence myself. I meant to keep myself as straight as I possibly could.

I had time only to run my course through my mind before the supper-bell was rung at the back door by Mrs. Fishley. Should I go in to supper as usual, and meet the whole family, including Ham? I answered this question in the affirmative, deciding that I would not sulk, or make any unnecessary trouble to any one. I went in, and took my seat as usual at the table, by the side of Flora. It was a very solemn occasion, for hardly a word was spoken during the meal. If I had been ugly, I might have congratulated myself upon the sensation I had produced.

The head of the family sweetened his tea twice, and upset the milk-pitcher upon the table-cloth, which, under ordinary circumstances, would have brought forth some sharp criticisms from his wife; but Mrs. Fishley neglected to express her disapprobation of her spouse's carelessness, even in the mildest terms. All these things assured me that our host and hostess were busy thinking of the great event of the afternoon. The captain looked morose and savage, and Mrs. Fishley looked as though a new burden, or a new grief, had been added to her heavy load of worldly cares.

I half suspected that Captain Fishley was not entirely satisfied with the conduct of either his wife or his son. It was even possible that he had spoken to them in disapprobation of their course; but I had no means of knowing. It seemed to me that otherwise father, mother, and son would have joined in a general jaw at me, as they had often done before. Whatever good or evil had been wrought by my vigorous action, my appetite was not impaired. I ate a hearty supper, and then went into the store for the mail-bag, which was to be carried down to Riverport.

"Are you going after the mail, Buck?" asked Captain Fishley, in an ugly, taunting tone, which assured me that he had not recovered from the shock.

"Yes, sir."

"O, you are! I didn't know but you would give up work altogether," sneered he, apparently disappointed to find me no longer a rebel.

"I told you I should do my work just as I always did. All I want is fair treatment for my sister and myself," I replied in the least offensive tones I could command.

"I expect my brother, Squire Fishley, will come up to-night," added the captain, more mildly. "You will go to the hotel in Riverport for him, and bring him up. Take a lantern with you; it will be dark to-night."

Squire Fishley had been a state senator, and the captain regarded him as one of the greatest men in Wisconsin. I was rather pleased to have his company home on the lonely ride from Riverport, and I confess that I was somewhat proud of making the acquaintance of the distinguished gentleman.

"Don't be in a hurry, Buck," said Ham Fishley, as I picked up the mail-bag.

I stopped and looked at him, for his tones were more conciliatory than I had heard him use within my remembrance. I actually flattered myself that I had conquered a peace.

"I want to ride with you as far as Crofton's," he added. "I have been very busy getting ready, and haven't had time to black my boots yet. It's a pretty stylish party I'm going to, and I want to look as scrumptious as any of them. Will you black them for me? I'll be much obliged to you if you will."

"Certainly I will, Ham, when you ask me in that way, and glad to do it for you," I replied, without hesitating an instant.

I took the boots and went to work upon them. There was an unmistakable smile of triumph on his face as I did so; but I was perfectly satisfied that the triumph was mine, not his. Doubtless those civil, polite words were an invention of the enemy, to win my compliance; and Ham, forgetting that I had not rebelled against the work, but only the tyrannical style of his order, was weak enough to believe that he had conquered me. I made up my mind to review the circumstances, and explain my position to him, on the way to Crofton's.

"Hasn't that letter come yet, Captain Fishley?" asked an ancient maiden lady, who entered the store while I was polishing Ham's boots.

"I haven't seen anything of it yet, Miss Larrabee," replied the postmaster.

"Dear me! What shall I do!" exclaimed the venerable spinster. "My brother, down in Ohio, promised to send me forty dollars; and I want the money awfully. I was going down to see Jim's folks, but I can't go, nor nothin', till that money comes. I hain't got nothin' to pay for goin' with, you see."

"I'm very sorry, Miss Larrabee. Perhaps the letter will come in to-night's mail," added the captain.

"But the mail don't git in till nine or ten o'clock, and that's after bedtime. Ethan writ me the money would be here by to-day, at the furthest. You don't suppose it's got lost—do you?"

"I think not. We've never lost anything in our office, leastwise not since I've been postmaster," answered Captain Fishley, who seemed to attribute the fact to his own superior management.

"It may come up to-night, as you say, and I will be down again in the morning to see about it," replied Miss Larrabee, as she left the store, hopeful that the money would arrive in season to enable her to depart the next day on her journey.

I finished blacking Ham's boots, and he put them on. He was going to a party at Crofton's, and had already dressed himself as sprucely as the resources of Torrentville would permit. He was seventeen years old, and somewhat inclined to be "fast." He was rather a good-looking fellow—an exceedingly good-looking fellow in his own estimation. Being an only son, his father and mother were disposed to spoil him, though not even Ham wholly escaped the sharp points and obliquities of his mother's temper. His father gave him what he believed to be a liberal allowance of spending money; but on this subject there was a disagreement between Ham and the "old man."

The young man always wanted more money, and the old man thought he had enough. Ham was pleasantly inclined towards some of the young ladies, and some of the young ladies were pleasantly inclined towards him. Ham liked to take them out to ride, especially Squire Crofton's youngest daughter, in the stable-keeper's new buggy; but his father thought the light wagon, used as a pleasure vehicle by the family, was good enough even for Elsie Crofton. I had heard some sharp disputes between them on this subject.

There was to be a party that evening at Crofton's. Ham was invited of course; I was not. Ham was considered a young man. I was deemed a boy, not competent to go to parties yet. As long as Flora could not go, I was content to stay at home with her.

I placed the mail-bag in the wagon, Ham took his seat by my side, and I drove off. As the reader already knows my position in regard to my tyrants, I need not repeat what passed between Ham and me. I told him I had made up my mind to do all the work I had been in the habit of doing, without grumbling, until October, but that I would not be treated like a dog any longer; I would take to the woods and live like a bear before I would stand it. My remarks were evidently very distasteful to my companion. He did not say much, and I was sorry to see that he was nursing his wrath against me. He regarded me as a being vastly inferior to himself, and the decided stand I had taken filled him with the same kind of indignation which a brutal teamster feels towards his contrary horse.

"Hold on a minute, Buck; I want to get a drink of water," said Ham, as we approached a spring by the roadside, half a mile before we reached Crofton's.

I drew up the black horse, and he jumped out of the wagon. He did not drink more than a swallow; and I did not think he was very thirsty.

"Go ahead!" said he, leaping into the rear of the wagon, behind the seat, where I had thrown the mail-bag.

He sat down on the end-board of the wagon, and though I thought it a little strange that he should take such an uncomfortable seat, especially when he had on his best clothes, I did not suspect any mischief. The first thing I knew after I had started the horse, the mail-bag came down upon my head with a force which made me see more stars than ever before twinkled in the firmament of my imagination. At the next instant, Ham seized me by the collar of my coat with both hands, in such a way that I could not easily move.

"Now, Buck Bradford, we'll settle this business. I'm going to know who's master, you or I," cried Ham.

"All right, Ham; you shall know in about two minutes and a half," I replied, choking with wrath, as I hauled in the horse.

Then commenced a struggle which it is impossible to describe. I do not myself know what I did, only that I thrashed, squirmed, and twisted till I found myself behind the seat with my antagonist; but he held on to my coat-collar as though his salvation depended upon the tenacity of his grip. Finally I doubled myself up, and came out of my coat. In the twinkling of an eye, I sprang upon him, and tumbled him out of the wagon, into the dirt of the road. Though he was a year older and two inches taller than I was, while he had been clerking it in the store, I had been nursing my muscles with the shovel and the hoe, the pitchfork and the axe; and I was the stronger and tougher of the two. I could do more, and bear more, than he. A fight depends as much upon the ability to endure injury as it does to inflict it.

The rough usage I had given Ham was very disheartening to him; while I, with the exception of being a little shaky about the head from the blow of the mail-bag, was as fresh as ever.

"Have you found out who's master yet, Ham?" I demanded, edging up to him.

He looked sheepish, and retreated a pace at every step I advanced. At this point, however, the black horse started, and I was obliged to abandon the field for a moment to attend to him, for the reins had fallen under his feet. I turned the horse around, and then I saw that my cowardly assailant had armed himself with a club.

CHAPTER V.

A BATTLE AT LONG RANGE.

I WAS always very fond of a dog and a horse, and had a taste for everything appertaining to these animals. Darky, as the black horse was called, and my dog Bully, were prime favorites with me. If I bore a divided love, it was so equally divided that I could not tell which I liked the best. I was fond of working over the horse, the wagon, the harnesses, and most especially I had a decided *penchant* for a graceful whip; but I wish to protest, in the same breath, that I never used it upon Darky. Though I was a firm believer in corporal punishment for vicious boys and vicious horses, I did not think he ever needed it. I had a suspicion that Ham Fishley had never had half enough of it, owing to the fact that he was a spoiled child. It seemed to me then that a good opportunity had come to supply the deficiency, even if it were administered strictly in self-defence.

When I had turned Darky, and admonished him to stand still, I saw that Ham had picked up a club, which appeared to be a broken cart-stake. It was necessary that I should provide for this new emergency. I glanced at the wagon, to see if there was anything about it that would answer my purpose. My eye fell upon the whip, which rested in the socket at the end of the seat. It was a very elegant whip in my estimation, with a lash long enough to drive a four-horse team. The brilliant thought occurred to me that this whip was better than a cart-stake for my present purpose, and I took it from its place.

I wish to say, most emphatically, in this connection, that I am not a fighting character; but, in the present instance, I was obliged to fight or submit to the most degrading abuse. Ham was in the act of asserting his right, not to ask me, but to order me, in the most offensive manner, to black his boots, or to perform other menial offices for him. I trust that I have already proved my willingness to do my duty, and to oblige even those whom I regarded as my enemies. Ham had made a cowardly assault upon me, and with the club in his hand he proposed to reduce me to what he considered a proper state of subjection.

I purposed that he should not reduce me at all. I walked towards the place where he stood, with the whip in my hand. As I approached him he moved towards me with his weapon thrown back in readiness to hit me. I halted first, and then retreated a few paces, to afford me time to disengage the lash from the handle of the whip,—I used to consider myself very skilful with the whip,—though this may be vanity,—and I could take a piece out of a maple leaf at twelve feet, three times out of four, all day long. This was one of my accomplishments as a boy, and I enjoyed the practice.

Retreating before the advance of Ham, I brought the whip smartly around the calves of his legs, with a regular coachman's flourish. This did not operate to cool my antagonist's temper; indeed, I am forced to confess that this was not exactly the way to subdue his ire. I am sorry to say that Ham used some naughty words, which politeness will not permit me to repeat. Then he rushed forward with redoubled energy, and I gave him another crack with the whip, which hit him in the tenderest part of his pedestals.

I knew by his wrinkled brow that the part smarted; but, as long as it did not cure him of the infatuation of "licking" me, I felt that he was responsible for all consequences. He wanted to throw himself upon me with that club, and I am satisfied that a single blow of the formidable weapon would have smashed my head. He followed up his treatment, and I followed up mine, keeping just out of the reach of his stick, and lathering his legs with the hard silk snapper of my whip.

He foamed, fretted, and struggled to gain the advantage of me; but he was mad, and I was cool, and I kept my respectful distance from him, punishing him as rapidly as I could swing the long lash. Ham soon became fearfully disgusted. At the rate he was subduing me, he must have felt that it would be a long job. His patience—not very carefully nursed—gave out at last; and, when he found that it would be impossible for him to inflict a single blow upon me, he raised the club, and let it fly at my head. If it had hit me there, I think the reader would have been saved the trouble of reading my adventures "Down the River." As it was, it struck me on the left shoulder, and I did not get over the effects of the blow for a fortnight. But I was too proud to show any signs of pain, or even to let him know that I had been hit.

I picked up the club, and held it in my left hand, to prevent him from making any further use of it, leaving my right to manipulate the whip. I felt that I had disarmed and overpowered him; but I was not yet quite content with his frame of mind, and I continued my favorite exercise for some time longer. I did not actually punish him any more; I only cracked the whip in unpleasant proximity to his tender extremities. He hopped and leaped like a Winnebago chief in the war-dance.

"Quit, Buck Bradford!" cried he, in tones of anguish.

"You have got enough of it—have you, Ham Fishley?" I replied, suspending the exercise.

"We'll settle this another time," howled he.

"No, we won't; we'll settle it now. You began it, and I want it finished now," I added, cracking the whip once more in the neighborhood of his pedal extremities.

"Quit—will you!"

"I will quit when you say you have had enough of it."

"You won't hear the last of this very soon, I can tell you!"

"What are you going to do about it, Ham?"

"I'll pay you off for it yet!"

"Will you!" I continued, startling his sensibilities again with the noise of the snapper.

"Yes, I will!" snarled he, passionately.

If the calf of his left leg had been a maple leaf at that moment, I should have taken a piece out of it as big as a dime.

"Mind out, Buck Bradford!"

"Have you had enough?" I demanded.

"Yes, I have!"

"O, well, if you are satisfied, I am, though you are not very good-natured about it. Next time you want to hit me over the head with the mail-bag, just remember that when I am awake I keep my eyes open," I replied, coiling up the lash of my whip. "When I told you I had stood this thing long enough, I got myself ready for anything that might come. I'm ready for anything more, and I shall be ready the next time you want to try it on."

"You had better go along with the mail," snapped he, in a tone so like his mother's that I could not have told who spoke if I had not seen Ham before me.

"I made this stop to accommodate you, not myself. After what has happened, I want to tell you once more, that I am ready to do my work like a man, and to treat you and everybody else like gentlemen, if you use me decently. If you know how to behave like a gentleman, I'd like to have you try it on for a few days, just to see how it would seem. If you will only do that, I promise you shall have no reason to complain of me. That's all I've got to say."

"You've said enough, and you had better go along with the mail," growled he.

I turned Darky again, very much to that knowing animal's dissatisfaction apparently, for my singular proceedings had doubtless impressed him with the idea that he was to escape his regular trip to Riverport.

"Aren't you going along to Crofton's?" I called to Ham, as I got into the wagon.

"A pretty fix I'm in to go to a party," replied he, as he glanced in disgust at his soiled garments.

"Well, you ought to have thought of that before you began the sport," I added, consolingly.

Ham made no reply, but fell vigorously to brushing his clothes with his hands.

"Better come along with me, Ham," I continued, kindly; for I felt that I could afford to be magnanimous; and I think one ought to be so, whether he can afford it or not.

"I'm not going to Crofton's in this fix," said he.

"I can help you out, if you like, Ham. I don't bear any ill will towards you, and just as lief do you a good turn as not," I added, taking from the box of the wagon-seat a small hand broom, which I kept there to dust off the cushion, and brush down the mail-bag after a dusty trip.

I jumped down from the wagon again, and moved towards him. He was shy of me after what had happened, and retreated at my approach.

"Let me brush your clothes, Ham. I won't hurt you."

"You have brushed me about enough already," said he, shaking his head.

"What are you afraid of?"

"I'm not afraid."

"Let me brush you, then. I wouldn't hurt you now any more than I would my own sister."

He stood still, and I brushed and rubbed his garments till he looked as bright and fresh as if he came out of the bureau drawer.

"There, you are all right now," I added, when I had finished the job. "Jump into the wagon, and I will take you along to Crofton's."

"You are up to some trick, Buck," said he, suspiciously.

"No, I'm not. I'm not afraid of you. I don't hit a fellow over the head with a mail-bag," I replied, seating myself in the wagon again.

Half a dozen "fellows and girls" were approaching from the direction of the village; and, as Ham did not care to see company just yet, he got into the wagon, and I drove off. He kept one eye on me all the time, and seemed to be afraid that I intended to continue the battle by some underhand measures.

"I am sorry this thing has happened, Ham; but I couldn't help it," I began, after we had ridden a quarter of a mile in silence. "You pitched in, and I had to defend myself. I hope you won't do it again."

Ham made no reply.

"Because, if you do, it will come out just as this has," I continued. "I suppose you feel a little sore about this scrape, for you don't come out first-best in it. You know that as well as I do. I reckon you won't want to talk much to the fellows about it. I don't blame you for not wanting to, Ham. But what I was going to say was this: if you don't say anything about it, I shall not."

"I don't know what I shall do," replied he, doggedly.

"I don't, either; but, between you and me, Ham, I don't think you feel much like bragging over it. If you don't mention it, I won't."

"I suppose you mean by that, you don't want me to say anything to the old man about it," growled he, involuntarily putting himself in the attitude of a conqueror, and me in that of a supplicant.

"No, Ham; that isn't what I meant. If you want to tell your father or anybody else of it, I'm willing; but one story's good till another's told. That's all."

Our arrival at Crofton's prevented any further consideration of the matter. Ham leaped out of the wagon without another word, rushed through the front gate, and disappeared, while I drove on towards Riverport.

CHAPTER VI.

SQUIRE FISHLEY.

HAM was quick-tempered, and I hoped he would get over the vindictive feelings which he manifested towards me. At the same time, I could not help thinking that he was fully in earnest when he told me I had not seen the end of it. Of Ham's moral attributes the least said would be the soonest mended. Certainly he was not a young man of high and noble purposes, like Charley Woodworth, the minister's son. Captain Fishley himself, as I had heard Clarence say, and as I knew from what I had seen and heard myself, was given to low cunning and overreaching. If he could make a dollar, he made it, and did not stand much upon the order of his making it.

I cannot say that he put prairie sand into the sugar, or put an ounce bullet into the side of the scale which contained the goods; but some people accused him of these things, and from what I knew of the man I could not believe that he was above such deeds. Ham was an apt scholar, and improved upon the precept and example of his father. I had heard him brag of cheating the customers, of mean tricks put upon the inexperience of women and children. If he had been a young man of high moral purposes, I might have hoped that we had seen the end of our quarrel.

I could not help thinking of this subject during the rest of my ride to Riverport, and I could not get rid of a certain undefined dread of consequences in the future. I criticise Ham and his father in the light of my own after experience rather than from any settled opinions which I had at the time; and I don't wish it to be understood that I was any better myself than I ought to be. I had no very distinct aspirations after goodness and truth. My character had not been formed. My dear little sister was my guide and Mentor. If I did wrong, she wept and prayed for me; and I am sure she saved me from many an evil deed by the sweet influence of her pure and holy life. If I had drank in more of her gentle spirit, the scene between Ham and myself could not have transpired.

I reached the post-office in Riverport, and took the mail-bag for Torrentville into the wagon, leaving the one I had brought down. Then I drove to the hotel, and inquired for Squire Fishley. The landlord told me that he was engaged with a party of gentlemen in a private room. Fortunately I was in no hurry, for I could not think of disturbing a person of so much consequence as Squire Fishley. I never reached home with the mail till nine o'clock, and the bag was not opened till the next morning, when sorting the mail was Ham's first business. I drove Darky into a shed, and amused myself by looking around the premises.

I walked about for half an hour, and then asked the landlord to tell Squire Fishley that I was waiting to take him up to his brother's. I was told that my passenger was just going down to the boat to see some friends off, and directed to put the squire's trunk into the wagon, and drive down to the steamboat landing. The landlord conducted me into the entry, and there, for the first time, I saw the captain's brother. He would have been a good-looking man under ordinary circumstances, but he was as boozy as an owl!

I was astonished, shocked, at this spectacle; for, unlike politicians in general, Squire Fishley had made his reputation, and his political capital, on his high moral and religious character. I had often heard what a good man the distinguished senator was, and I was horrified at seeing him drunk. With unsteady gestures, and in maudlin tones, he pointed out his trunk to me, and I put it into the wagon. I did not see him again till he reached the steamboat landing. He went on board with two other gentlemen, and was absent another half hour.

The bell of the steamer rang furiously for the start, and I began to be afraid that my passenger's devotion to his friends would lead him to accompany them down the river. I went up into the cabin, and found him taking a "parting drink" with them. I told him the boat was just starting; he hastily shook hands with his companions, and accompanied me down to the plank. I crossed it, and had hardly touched the shore before I heard a splash behind me. I turned, and saw that Squire Fishley had toppled into the river. His last dram appeared to be the ounce that had broken the camel's back.

I saw the current bear him under the guards of the boat, where, in the darkness, he was lost to my view. I ran, followed by a dozen idlers, to the stern of the boat, and presently the helpless tippler appeared again. A raft of floating logs lay just below the steamer. I cast off the up-stream end of one of them, and the current swung it out in the river. Leaping astride it, I pushed off, just in time to intercept the unfortunate senator, who had sense enough left to grasp it.

"Hold on tight, squire!" I cried to him.

I worked along the log to the place where he was, and assured myself that he had a secure hold. Beyond keeping myself afloat, I was as helpless as he was, for I could not do anything to guide or propel our clumsy bark. We had disappeared from the view of the people on shore, for the night was, as Captain Fishley had predicted, very dark.

I think we floated half a mile down the river, and I heard persons shouting far above us, in boats. We were approaching a bend in the stream, where I hoped the current would set us near enough to the shore to enable me to effect a landing. Just then the steamer came puffing along; but her course took her some distance from us. She passed us, and in the swell caused by her wheels we were tossed up and down, and I was afraid the squire would be shaken from his hold. I grasped him by the collar with one hand, and kept him in position till the commotion of the water had partially subsided.

But the swell did us a good turn, for it drove the log towards the shore, at the bend of the stream, and I found that I could touch bottom. With a hold for my feet, I pushed the timber towards the bank till one end of it grounded. I then helped the squire to walk up the shoaling beach, out of the river. Cold water is the natural enemy of ardent spirits, and in this instance it had gained a partial victory over its foe, for the squire was nearly sobered by his bath.

"This is bad—very bad!" said my passenger, when he had shaken some of the water from his garments.

"I know it is, Squire Fishley; but we have got over the worst of it," I replied.

"I'm afraid not, boy. I shall never get over the disgrace of it," he added, with a shudder—partly from cold, I judged, and partly from a dread of consequences.

"Nobody will know anything about it if you don't tell of it. When you fell in, I heard a dozen people ask who you were, and nobody could tell."

"Don't let any one see me, boy," pleaded he, as we heard the voices of people moving down the bank of the river in search of the unfortunate.

I knew just where we were, and I conducted him to an old lumber shed, some distance from the bank of the river, where I left him to go for the horse and wagon. I avoided the people who were searching for the unfortunate, and found Darky just where I had hitched him, at the steamboat landing. I was not very uncomfortable, for I had not been all over into the water. I drove down to the lumber shed, took the squire in, and headed towards home. The senator was shivering with cold, though fortunately it was a very warm day for the season, and he did not absolutely suffer.

It had been cloudy and threatening rain all the afternoon and evening, and before we reached the main road it began to pour in torrents. I had an oil-cloth, which I put over the trunk and the mail. Under ordinary circumstances, a seven-mile ride in such a heavy rain would have been a great misfortune; but, as both of us had been in the river, it did not make much difference to us. I had no umbrella; and it would have done no good if I had, the wind was so fresh, and the storm so driving. If we had not been wet in the beginning, we should have been soaked to the skin long before we reached Torrentville.

The squire suffered so much from cold that I advised him to get out, take hold of the back of the wagon, and walk or run a mile or so to warm up his blood. He took my advice, and improved his condition very much. But the cold was by no means the greatest of his troubles. Remorse, or, more likely, the fear of discovery, disturbed him more.

"Boy, what is your name?" asked he, after he had walked his mile, and was able to speak without shivering.

"John Buckland Bradford, sir; but the folks all call me Buck."

"You seem to be a very smart boy, Buck, and you have done me a good turn to-night, which I shall never forget."

"I'm glad I helped you, sir. I would have done as much as that for anybody."

"It is bad, very bad," added he, apparently thinking of the consequences.

"I know it is, sir. That was a pretty narrow plank on the steamboat."

"It wasn't the narrow plank," he replied, bitterly.

"I suppose you had been taking a little too much," I added, willing to help him out.

"Did you think I was intoxicated?"

"I don't know much about it, but I did think so."

"I would rather give a thousand dollars than have it known that I drank too much and fell into the river. The story would ruin me, and spoil all my prospects."

Squire Fishley was a stranger in Riverport. He had not been to Torrentville since I lived with the captain, and I was sure no one knew who it was that had fallen into the river. I comforted him, and assured him it would be all right.

"If your friends on board of the steamer don't expose you, no one else will," I continued.

"They will not; they are going to New Orleans, and will not return for months. If you should happen to say anything to my brother or his family—"

"I will not breathe it," I interposed.

"I will do something handsome for you, Buck, and be your best friend."

"I don't mind that," I replied.

"I am not in the habit of drinking ardent spirits, or even wine, to excess, when I am at home, though I don't belong to the temperance society," said he. "I didn't take much, and my friends would not let me off. I don't know that I ever was really intoxicated before in my life."

"It is a bad habit."

"But it is not my habit, and I mean to stop drinking entirely," he replied, earnestly; and I could not help thinking how humiliating it must be for a great man like him to confess his folly to such a poor boy as I was.

"We are nearly home now, sir," said I, after we had ridden a while in silence.

"You will remember your promise—won't you, Buck?"

"Certainly I will, sir."

"Take this," he added, crowding something into my hand.

"What is it, sir?" I asked.

"No matter now; it may help your memory."

It was a little roll of wet paper, and I thrust it into my pocket as I drove into the yard.

CHAPTER VII.

AFTER MIDNIGHT.

ALTHOUGH it was after eleven o'clock, Captain Fishley and his wife were still up, waiting for the arrival of the distinguished guest.

"Now, remember," said Squire Fishley, as I drove into the yard, and the captain came out at the back door.

"Don't be at all afraid of me," I replied.

"How are you, Moses?" exclaimed Captain Fishley, as, by the light of the lantern he carried in his hand, he saw that his brother had arrived.

"Pretty well, I thank you; but very wet and cold," answered the squire, shivering.

"Well, I am glad to see you," added the postmaster, as he took the hand of the guest and helped him out of the wagon.

The squire was so chilled that he could hardly stand. So far as I could judge, he had entirely recovered from his debauch. The captain led the way into the house, and I followed them with the trunk and the mail-bag. Mrs. Fishley bestowed a cordial welcome upon her brother-in-law, and placed the rocking-chair before the stove, in which there was still a good fire.

"Why, you are as wet as though you had been in the river!" cried Mrs. Fishley.

"It has been raining very hard," replied the squire, casting an anxious glance at me.

"What made you so late?" asked the captain. "I expected you by nine o'clock."

"I had some friends with me who were on the way to New Orleans, and I waited to see them off," answered the senator, with a shudder—not at the thought of his friends, perhaps, but on account of the chill which pervaded his frame.

"You'll catch your death a cold, Moses," interposed Mrs. Fishley. "I think you'd better take something, to guard against the chills."

"Yes; I'll give you a glass of corn whiskey, mixed with hot water," added the captain, taking up the suggestion.

"No, I think I won't take any," replied the squire, shaking his head.

"Hadn't you better?" persisted Mrs. Fishley. "It'll do you a heap of good."

"Not to-night, thank you!"

"I don't believe in drinkin' liquor when a body's well; but when they're wet through, and shiverin' with cold as you are, Moses, it is good for 'em—only as a medicine, you know."

But not even as a medicine could Squire Fishley be induced to partake of any of the fire-water. He had drank corn whiskey enough for one day; and I think at that moment he loathed the thought of drinking it. He compromised the matter, being a politician, by offering to drink a dish of hot tea, which, I doubt not, was just as good for him as the "ardent" would have been.

I warmed my fingers a little at the stove, and then went out to take care of Darky. I stirred my own blood by the exercise of rubbing him down; and, when I left him, nicely blanketed, I think he was as comfortable as the squire in the house, and I am sure his head did not ache half so badly. My work for the night was done; but, before I went into the house, I could not help taking the present which the senator had given me from my pocket and examining it. I had suspected, from the first, that it was a bank bill. I thought that the squire had given me a dollar or two to deepen the impression upon my memory, and I had already come to the conclusion that he was a more liberal man than his brother; as, indeed, he could afford to be, for he was said to be quite wealthy.

I took the little roll from my pocket while up in the hay-loft, where I had gone to give Darky his last feed. It was wet, but the paper was new and strong, and had sustained no serious injury. I unrolled the bills, and was astonished to find there were not less than half a dozen of them. As they had apparently just come from the bank, they stuck together very closely. The first bill was a one, the next a five; and by this time I was amazed at the magnitude of the sum, for I had never before had six dollars of my own in my hand.

I looked further, and was utterly overwhelmed when I found that each of the other four bills was a ten. Forty-six dollars! Squire Fishley had certainly made a mistake. He could not have intended to give me all that money. Befuddled and befogged by the whiskey and the cold bath, he must have forgotten that the roll contained forty-six dollars, instead of two or three, which was probably all he intended to give me. I should have felt rich with a couple of dollars; but actually possessed of the sum in my hand, I should have been a John Jacob Astor in my own estimation.

The money was not mine. The squire had not intended to give me all that, and it would not be right for me to keep it. I could not help thinking that if I chose to keep the money, I might do so with impunity. I had the squire's secret, and he would not dare to insist upon my returning the bills; but this would be mean, and I concluded that I should feel better with the two or three dollars fairly obtained than if I took advantage of the obvious blunder of the giver.

"What have you got there, Buck?"

I started as though a rifle ball had struck me. Turning, I saw Ham Fishley standing at the head of the stairs, and I wondered how he had been able to come up the steps without my hearing him. I had been intensely absorbed in the contemplation of the bills, and was lost to everything around me. If I had heard any noise, I supposed it was Darky. I saw that Ham had taken off his boots, and put on a pair of old rubbers, which explained why I had not heard his step on the stairs.

"What have you got there, Buck?" repeated he, as I did not answer the first question.

"I've got a little money," I replied.

"Where did you get it?"

"I didn't steal it?"

"Well, I didn't say you did. I only asked you a civil question."

"It's some money I made on my own account," I replied, as composedly as I could.

"Have you done with that lantern? I want it," he continued, either satisfied with my answer, or too wet and cold to pursue the inquiry any further.

I gave him the lantern, and followed him down stairs, greatly annoyed by the discovery he had made, for I could not help thinking that he had been watching me, perhaps to obtain another opportunity of settling the old score. I closed the stable door, and went into the house. The family, including the squire, had gone to bed. Ham, with the lantern in his hand, passed through the entry into the shop. I lighted a lamp in the kitchen, and went up to my room, which was in the L over the store. I took off my wet clothes, put on a dry shirt, and got into bed.

Though it was after midnight, I could not at once go to sleep. I could not help thinking of the stirring events of the evening, for never before had so much happened to me in so brief a period. I was beginning to gape fearfully, and to lose myself, when the whinings of Bully at the side door disturbed me. My canine friend usually slept in the barn; but he appeared to have been out late, like the rest of us, and had been locked out. He was a knowing dog, and the light in the store had probably assured him that some one was up, or he would not have had the impudence to apply for admission at that unseemly hour.

I had just become comfortably warm in bed, and did not like the idea of getting up, even for the accommodation of Bully, though I was willing to do so rather than oblige the poor fellow to stay out in the cold all night. I waited a while to see if Ham would not have the grace to admit my friend; but the whining continued, and reluctantly I jumped out of bed. Putting on my socks and pants, I crept down stairs, so as not to disturb the squire, who occupied the front chamber.

In the lower entry, I found that the door which led to the shop was partly open; and I looked in as I went along, for I wondered what Ham was about at that late hour. He was sorting the mail, which I had brought up from Riverport, and I concluded that he intended to lie abed late in the morning. I paused a moment at the door, and soon became satisfied that he was doing something more than sorting the mail. He was not ten feet from me, and I could distinctly observe his operations.

I should not have staid an instant after I found what he was doing if his movements had not excited my attention. He had lighted the large hanging lamp over the counter where the mail was sorted; and, as I was about to pass on to the relief of Bully, I saw him hold a letter up to the light, as if to ascertain its contents. I could not entirely make out the direction upon it; but, as he held it up to the lamp, peering in at the end, I saw that the capital letter commencing the last name was an L. I concluded that this must be the letter for which Miss Larrabee had inquired, and which she had declared was to contain forty dollars.

Ham glanced around the store; but, as I was in the darkness of the entry, and concealed by the door, he did not see me. He was nervous and shaky in his movements. He held the letter up to the light again, and having apparently satisfied himself that it contained a valuable enclosure, he broke it open. I confess that I was filled with horror, and, of the two, I was probably more frightened than he was. I saw him take several bank bills from the paper and thrust them into his pocket. I had never considered Ham capable of an act so wicked as this. I was shocked and confounded. I did not know what to do. Badly as he had treated me, I would gladly have saved him from such a gross crime as that he was committing.

What should I do? What could I do? I was on the point of rushing into the store, telling him I had seen the flagrant act, and begging him to undo the deed by restoring the money to the letter, and sealing it again. At that instant he lighted a match, and set the letter on fire. I was too late. He took the burning paper in his hand, carried it to the stove, and threw it in. He waited a moment till it was consumed, and then returned to the mail counter. The envelope still lay there; he carried that to the stove, and saw it ignited from the burning letter.

HAM FISHLEY'S CRIME

Ham's nefarious work appeared to be finished; and, without being able to decide what I should do, I hurried back to my chamber, even forgetting all about poor Bully in my agitation. I heard the step of Ham a moment later. The whining of the dog attracted his attention, and he let him in before he went to his room. My heart beat as though I had robbed the mail myself. I trembled for Ham. Though he had always been overbearing and tyrannical in his demeanor towards me; though he had taken a mean and cowardly advantage of me that evening; though he was a young man whom I could not like,—yet I had lived in the same house with him for several years, and known him ever since I came to Torrentville. I did not wish anything so bad to come upon him as that he was bringing upon himself. It was sad and pitiful enough to be mean and tyrannical, without being a thief and a robber.

I really pitied Ham, and if he had not destroyed the letter, I should have gone to him, and begged him to retrace his steps. I knew him too well to take such a course now, and I lay thinking of his crime, till, overcome with weariness, I went to sleep.

CHAPTER VIII.

MISS LARRABEE'S LETTER.

IF I did not get up as early as usual the next morning, none of my tyrants were stirring in season to abuse me for lying abed so late; for they, like myself, had not retired until after midnight. The first thing that came to my mind in the morning was the scene I had witnessed in the post-office. The secret seemed to burn in my soul, and I wanted some means of getting rid of it. I actually pitied Ham, and would gladly have availed myself of any method of saving him from the crime—of saving him from himself, rather than from the penalty of the offence, for even then the crime seemed to me to be worse than the punishment, and more to be dreaded.

It was nearly breakfast time when Ham made his appearance, and I imagined that he had found some difficulty in going to sleep with the burden of his crime resting upon his conscience. Squire Fishley did not appear till the family were just ready to sit down at the table. He looked sleepy, stupid, and ashamed of himself, and Mrs. Fishley thought he must have taken cold. According to his custom, the senator said grace at the table, by invitation of his brother, who, however, never returned thanks himself.

I could not help keeping one eye fixed on the distinguished man, for so unusual an event as saying grace in that house did not fail to make an impression upon me. I noticed that he cast frequent glances at me, and very uneasy ones at that. Doubtless he felt that I could unfold a tale which was not exactly consistent with his religious pretensions. But, in spite of all I knew, I did not regard him as a hypocrite. I did not know enough about him to enable me to reach so severe a judgment. The shame and penitence he had manifested assured me he was not in the habit of getting intoxicated; and I was willing to believe that he had been led away by the force of circumstances a single time, and that the error would cure itself by its own reaction.

"It's rather chilly this morning," said Captain Fishley. "Buck, you may make a little fire in the stove."

"It has cleared off pleasant, and it will be warmer by and by, when the sun gets up," added Mrs. Fishley, who always had something to say, on every possible topic that could be introduced, whether she knew anything about it or not.

I went to the store. In the open stove were the tindered remains of the letter Ham had burned. The sheet of paper had been entirely consumed; but the envelope, which he had destroyed afterwards, was only half burned. The right hand lower corner had apparently been wet, so that it resisted the action of the fire, and appeared to rise in judgment against the mail robber. The piece contained part of the last name of the superscription, with a portion of the town, county, and state, of the address. Without any definite purpose in doing so, I put the remains of the envelope in my pocket.

While I was making the fire, Miss Larrabee entered the store, and went up to the counter appropriated to the post-office. Ham whistled Yankee Doodle, which was patriotic enough, but out of place even in the shop, and sauntered leisurely over to wait upon her. I was astonished to see how cool he was; but I think the whistle had a deceptive effect.

"Has that letter come yet?" asked Miss Larrabee; and her anxiety was visible in the tones of her voice.

"What letter do you mean, Miss Larrabee?" asked Ham, suspending his whistle, and looking as blank as though he had never heard of it.

"Why, the letter I came for last night," replied the ancient maiden.

"For yourself?"

"Yes; the letter from Ethan's folks."

"I haven't heard anything about it before."

"Well, you was a standin' here last night when I axed your father for it," added Miss Larrabee, who thought the matter was of consequence enough to have everybody take an interest in it.

"I didn't mind what you said. So many letters come here, that I can't keep the run of them."

"I've axed your father for't goin' on three times; and he said it would come in last night's mail. It must have come afore this time."

"If it must, I suppose it has," replied Ham, taking a pile of letters from the pigeon-hole marked L.

Having lighted the kindlings in the stove, I stood up to observe the conduct of Ham. He resumed his whistle, and examined the letters. Of course he did not find the one he was looking for.

"None for Larrabee," said he, suspending the patriotic air long enough to utter the words.

"Goodness gracious! There must be!" exclaimed the unhappy spinster. "Have you looked 'em all over?"

"I have."

But Ham took down the L's again, and went through the pile once more.

"None for Larrabee," he repeated, and then, for variety's sake, whistled the first strain of Hail, Columbia.

"But, Mr. Fishley, there must be a letter for me. Ethan writ me there was one comin'; and he said it would be here by to-day, for sartain," protested Miss Larrabee. "Mebbe it's got into some other hole."

"Well, to please you, I'll look them all over; but I don't remember seeing any letter for you."

"I tell ye it must have come afore now," persisted the venerable maiden.

Ham whistled his favorite air as he went through all the letters in the pigeon-holes, from A to Z. He did not find it, and Miss Larrabee was in despair. She had made all her preparations to visit "Jim's folks," and had intended to start that day.

"It's a shame!" exclaimed she. "I know Ethan sent the letter. He wouldn't play no sech trick on me. Them mail folks ought to look out for things better'n that."

"If it didn't come, it didn't," added Ham, consolingly.

"But I know it did come. Ethan must have put it in the post-office. 'Tain't like him to say he'd do a thing, and then not do it. I almost know he sent the letter."

At this point Captain Fishley and his brother entered the store, and Miss Larrabee appealed to him. The postmaster looked the letters over very carefully; but, as there was none for the lady, he couldn't find any. He was very sorry, but he displayed more philosophy than the spinster, and "bore up" well under the trial.

"What on airth am I to do!" ejaculated Miss Larrabee. "Here I've got all ready to go and see Jim's folks; but I can't go because I hain't got no money. When I set about doin' a thing, I want to do it."

"People sometimes make mistakes in directing their letters, and then they have to go to the dead-letter office," suggested Captain Fishley.

"Ethan didn't make no mistake. 'Tain't like him to make mistakes. Do you think Ethan don't know where I live?"

"I don't know anything about it, only that the letter isn't here."

"Dear suz! What shall I do? When a body's made up her mind to go, it's desp'ate aggravatin' not to go."

At this trying juncture, Squire Fishley interposed, and, after some inquiries in regard to the responsibility of the parties, suggested that his brother should lend the lady money enough to enable her to make her journey.

"I'd be much obleeged to you, Captain Fishley, if you'd do it," said Miss Larrabee, delighted with the suggestion. "I shan't be gone more'n a month, and when I come back I'll hand it to you. That letter must come to-day or to-morrow, and if you have a mind to, you can open it, and take the money out. It will save me the interest."

"But suppose the letter has gone to the dead-letter office?" added the postmaster.

"Sakes alive! I've got money enough to pay it, if the letter is lost. Why, Ethan's got more'n 'leven hundred dollars that belongs to me."

"All right, Miss Larrabee," replied Captain Fishley, as he took out the money, and wrote a note for the amount.

The worthy maiden of many summers put on her spectacles, signed the note, and counted the money. She was happy again, for the journey was not to be deferred. I think Ham was as glad to have her go as she was to go. I could not help watching him very closely after his father and the squire left the store, to observe how he carried himself in his course of deception and crime. I had never known him to whistle so much before, and I regarded it as the stimulus he used in keeping up his self-possession.

"What are you staring at me for, Buck Bradford?" demanded he, as I stood gazing across the counter at him.

"A cat may look at the king," I replied, stung by the harsh words, after I had cherished so many kind feelings towards him, though I forgot that I had not expressed them, since the affray on the road.

"Do I owe you anything?"

"No, you don't owe me anything."

"Yes, I do. I owe you something on last night's account, and I'm going to pay it too," he added, shaking his head at me in a threatening manner.

I did not like his style, and not wishing to make a disturbance in the store, I said nothing. I walked up to the stove, where I found that my fire was not doing very well, for my interest in the letter had caused me to neglect it. I put on some more kindlings, and then knelt down on the hearth to blow up the fire with my breath. Captain Fishley and the squire had left the store, and Ham and I were alone. I heard my youngest tyrant come from behind the counter; but I did not think anything of it. While I was kneeling on the hearth, and blowing up the failing embers with all my might, Ham came up behind me, with a cowhide in his hand, taken from a lot for sale, and before I suspected any treachery on his part, or had time to defend myself, he struck me three heavy blows, each of which left a mark that remained for more than a week.

I sprang to my feet; but the wretch had leaped over the counter, and fortified himself behind it. He looked as ugly as sin itself; but I could see that he was not without a presentiment of the consequences of his rash act. I do not profess to be an angel in the quality of my temper, and I was as mad as a boy of fifteen could be. I made a spring at him, and was going over the counter in a flying leap, when he gave me a tremendous cut across the shoulder.

"Hold on there, Buck Bradford!" called he, as he pushed me back with his left hand. "We are square now."

"No, we are not," I replied, taking a cowhide from a bundle of them on a barrel. "We have a new account to settle now."

"We are just even for what you gave me last night," said he.

"Not yet," I added, leaping over the counter in another place; and, rushing upon him, I brought my weapon to bear upon his shoulders.

"What are you about, you villain?" demanded Captain Fishley, returning to the store at this moment.

He seized me by the collar, and being a powerful man, he wrested the cowhide from my grasp, and before I could make any successful demonstration, he laid the weapon about my legs, till they were in no better condition than I had left Ham's the evening before.

"I'll teach you to strike my son!" said he, breathless with excitement.

"He struck me," I flouted.

"No matter if he did; you deserved it. Now go to the barn, and harness the horse."

I saw the squire coming into the store. I was overpowered; and, with my legs stinging with pain, I went to the barn.

CHAPTER IX.

THE HUNGRY RUNAWAY.

I WENT to the barn, but not to obey the order of Captain Fishley. I was as ugly as Ham himself, and anything more than that was needless. I went there because the barn was a sort of sanctuary to me, whither I fled when the house was too warm to hold me. I went there to nurse my wrath; to think what I should do after the new indignities which had been heaped upon me. I had not been the aggressor in the quarrel. I had been meanly insulted and assaulted.

After the blows of Captain Fishley, I felt that Torrentville was no place for me and for my poor sister. The six months which were to intervene before the coming of Clarence, and the end of my misery, looked like so many years to me. If it had not been for Flora, I would not have remained another hour in the house of my tyrants. I would have fled that moment.

I could not stay long in the barn without another row, for the captain had ordered me to harness the horse; and I concluded that he and the squire were going to ride. I was just ugly enough then to disobey; in fact, to cast off all allegiance to my tyrants. I felt as though I could not lift my finger to do anything more for them till some atonement for the past had been made. I gave Darky some hay, and then left my sanctuary, without knowing where I was going.

Back of the house, and half a mile from it, was a narrow but deep stream, which flowed into the creek. This branch ran through a dense swamp—the only one I knew of in that part of the state. In the early spring its surface was overflowed with water. It was covered with a thick growth of trees, and the place was as dismal, dark, and disagreeable as anything that can be imagined.

Hardly any one ever visited the swamp except myself. At this season of the year it was not possible to pass through it, except in a boat. I was rather fond of exploring out-of-the-way places, and this deep and dark morass had early attracted my attention. The year before I had made a small raft, and threaded its gloomy recesses with Sim

Gwynn, a stupid crony of mine, and, like myself, an orphan, living out and working for his daily bread.

When I left the barn, I wandered towards the swamp. I was thinking only of the indignities which had been heaped upon me. I meant to keep out of the way till dinner-time. At the foot of the slope, as I descended to the low land, I came across the raft on which Sim and I had voyaged through the avenues of the dismal swamp the preceding year. It was in a dilapidated condition; and, after adjusting the boards upon the logs, I pushed off, and poled the clumsy craft into the depths of the thicket. The place was in harmony with my thoughts.

I continued on my purposeless voyage till I reached the swollen branch of the creek. Piled up at a bend of the stream was a heap of logs, planks, boards, and other fugitive lumber which had come down from the saw-mills, miles up in the country. I seated myself on this heap of lumber, to think of the present and the future. I noticed that one end of a log had been driven ashore by the current, and had caught between two trees. All the rest of the boards, planks, and timbers had rested upon this one, and being driven in by the current at the bend, had been entrapped and held by it.

This fact made me think of myself. My refusal to black Ham's boots the day before had been the first log, and all my troubles seemed to be piling themselves up upon it. I thought then, and I think now, that I had been abused. I was treated like a dog, ordered about like a servant, and made to do three times as much work as had been agreed with my guardian. I felt that it was right to resist. There was no one to fight my battle, and that of my poor sister, but myself. I am well aware that I took upon myself a great responsibility in deciding this question. Perhaps, without the counsel of my brother, I should not have dared to proceed as I did. Bad as the consequences threatened to be, I did not regret that I had permitted the log to drift ashore.

Again that pine stick seemed like some great vice, sin, or error, which, having thrown itself up from the current of life, soon gathers many other vices, sins, and errors around or upon it. As this log had caught a score of others, so one false step leads to more. The first glass of liquor, the first step in crime, the first unclean word, were typified in this stick.

I was not much of a philosopher or moralist then, but it seemed to me that the entire heap ought to be cleared away; that the whole course of the river might be choked by it in time, if the obstruction was not removed. By detaching that first log, all the rest would be cast loose, and carried away by the stream—just as I had known old Cameron to become an honest, Christian man by cutting away the log of intemperance. I was about to use my setting-pole for the purpose of detaching the obstacle, when I happened to think that the lumber might be saved—just as the zeal of Paul, in persecuting the Christians, was the same zeal that did so much to build up the true church.

Why should I trouble myself to save the lumber? It would cost a deal of hard labor, and Captain Fishley would be the only gainer. I decided at once not to waste my time for his benefit, and was on the point of detaching the mischievous stick which had seduced all the others, when I heard a voice calling my name. I was rather startled at first, thinking it might be one of my tyrants in search of me.

"Buck!" shouted the voice again; and I was satisfied it was not that of either of my oppressors. I could not see through the dense thicket of the swamp; but another repetition of the call assured me it came from Sim Gwynn, my fellow-navigator in the swamp.

"Come here, Buck—will you?" said he, when I had answered his summons.

"I'm coming, Sim!" I shouted.

I plied the pole vigorously, and soon propelled the raft to the place where he stood.

"I saw you come down here, Buck; and I waited for you a while," said he, stepping upon the raft at my invitation.

"Why didn't you sing out before, then?"

"I thought you'd be coming back," he replied, with more embarrassment in his manner than the circumstances seemed to warrant.

"Where do you want to go, Sim?" I asked, as I pushed off again.

"Anywhere; it don't make any difference to me now where I go," he answered, shaking his head.

"Why, what is the matter? Are you not at work now?"

"Not to-day. I've been waiting to see you, Buck."

"What for?"

"I left off work yesterday."

"What's up?"

"I wanted to see you, Buck."

He talked and acted very strangely, and I was sure something unusual had happened. He lived with a farmer by the name of Barkspear, who had the reputation of being the stingiest man in Torrentville, if not in the county. Sim was a great, stout, bow-legged fellow, as good-natured as the day was long. He always looked as though he had recently escaped from the rag-bag, with its odds and ends sticking to him. Though he always looked fat and hearty, he frequently complained that he could not get enough to eat at Barkspear's.

"What's the matter, Sim? Why don't you tell me what has happened?" I continued.

"I wanted to see you, Buck," he repeated, for the fourth time.

"What do you want to see me for?"

"Well, I thought I wanted to see you," said he, fumbling his fingers together, and looking into the water, instead of in my face.

"You do see me," I added, impatiently, beginning to have a suspicion that he had lost his senses, what little he had.

"I wanted to ask you something," he added, after a long pause.

"Well, ask it."

"I thought I would tell you about it, and that's the reason I wanted to see you," said Sim, poking about his trousers pockets, just as some boys do when they are going to make a speech in school.

"About what?" I asked, more mildly, when I saw that Sim was sort of choking, and exhibited some signs of an intention to break out in a fit of blubbering.

"I'm a poor boy. I haven't got many friends, and—and I wanted to see you."

This was too much for him, and, turning away his head, he cried like a great baby. I pushed the raft up to a fallen tree, whose trunk was above the water, and stuck the pole down into the mud, so as to keep it in place.

"What is the matter, Sim?" I asked again, seating myself on the log. "If I can help you any way, I will."

"I knew you would; and that's the reason I wanted to see you," blubbered Sim, seating himself by my side.

"You said you stopped work yesterday," I continued, in the kindest tones I could command, for I was much moved by his apparent distress.

"Yes; I stopped work yesterday, and—and—and that's the reason I wanted to see you," sobbed he, wiping his face with his dirty hands.

I thought he wanted to see me for a good many reasons; but I concluded to wait until he had recovered his self-possession before I asked any more questions. When the silence had continued for full five minutes, it became embarrassing to him, and he remarked that he had wanted to see me.

"I believe you have lost your senses, Sim," I replied.

"No; I haven't lost my senses—only my stomach," said he, with a piteous look, which alone prevented me from laughing at his ludicrous speech, and the more ludicrous expression upon his face.

"What is the matter with your stomach?" I inquired.

"Nothing in it," whined he.

"What do you mean?" I asked, sharply, rather to quicken his wits than to express anger.

"I quit work yesterday."

"So you said before."

"I can't stay to Barkspear's no longer; and that's the reason I wanted to see you," said he, blubbering, and absolutely howling in his deep grief.

"Why not?" I asked, gently.

"I didn't get hardly any breakfast yesterday morning," sobbed he; "only a crust of brown bread. But I wouldn't minded that, if there'd only been enough on't. I was working in the garden, and when I saw Mis' Barkspear go out to the barn to look for eggs, I went into the house. In the buttery I found a piece of cold b'iled pork, about as big as one of my fists—it was a pretty large piece!—and four cold taters. I eat the pork and taters all up, and felt better. That's what I wanted to see you for."

"Why did you quit work?"

"Mis' Barkspear saw me coming out of the house, and when she missed the pork and taters, she knowed I did it. She told the old man I'd eat up the dinner for that day. Barkspear licked me, and I quit. I hain't had nothin' to eat since," said he, bursting into tears.

I pushed the raft back to the landing-place again.

"You won't tell on me, Buck—will you?" pleaded he.

"No. I'm going to get you something to eat."

He was willing.

CHAPTER X.

WHAT SIM GWYNN WANTED TO SEE ME FOR.

SIM GWYNN was hungry, and that was the greatest misfortune which could possibly happen to him. He was growing rapidly, and consumed a vast amount of food. I pitied him, as I did any one who was kept on short allowance, and I hastened to the house as quickly as I could, in order to relieve what was positive suffering on his part. I intended to obtain the food at home if possible; if not, to purchase it at the store.

Captain Fishley had probably harnessed the horse himself, for he and the squire had gone away. I went into the house. No one was there but Flora. Mrs. Fishley had gone, with her husband, to sun herself in the smiles of the senator. She never liked to be left at home when there was anything going on. In the buttery I found plenty of cooked provisions; for, whatever else may be said of the Fishleys, they always had enough to eat, and that which was good enough. "Short provender" had never been one of my grievances, and I pitied poor Sim all the more on this account.

Mrs. Fishley had evidently given the distinguished visitor credit for a larger appetite than he possessed after his debauch the night before, and there was at least a pound of cold fried ham left. I took a paper bag, and put into it half the meat and as much cold corned beef as would have fed me for two days, with a plentiful supply of biscuits, crackers, and brown bread. I filled the bag full, determined that Sim should have plenty to eat for once in his life. Thus laden with enough to fill the stomach that had "nothing in it," I returned to the swamp.

I need not say that the hungry runaway was glad to see me. I pushed off the raft, and poled it over to the fallen tree, where we should not be disturbed by any possible passer-by. Sim looked piteously sad and sorrowful; he glanced wistfully at the paper bag, and seemed to begrudge every moment of delay. At the tree, I took out the contents of the bag, and spread them on the log. Sim's eyes dilated till they were like a pair of saucers, and an expression of intense satisfaction lighted up his dull features.

"Go in, Sim," said I, as soon as I had spread the table for him.

"Thank you, Buck! You are a good fellow," replied he, warmly. "I knowed you'd help me, and that's what I wanted to see you for."

I thought it would be cruel to interrupt an operation so agreeable to him as that of eating, and I asked no questions. He looked grateful, and satisfactorily demonstrated that the proof of the pudding is in the eating. Though I was amused at his greediness, and enjoyed his appetite almost as much as he did himself, I did not wish to embarrass him; and, mounting the fallen tree, I walked upon its trunk so far from him that it was not convenient for him to speak to me. He had it all his own way; for I think it is mean to watch a hungry boy when he is eating, or to take note of the quantity he consumes.

From my position I could see the stream, and the pile of lumber over which I had moralized. I could not help thinking that something must be done with those refuse logs and boards. I cannot exactly explain how it was, but that pile of senseless lumber seemed, in some indefinite manner, to connect itself with my affairs at the house. The thrashing I had just received from my two masculine tyrants assured me that I was no match for both of them. In a word, it was strongly impressed upon my mind that I could not stay in Torrentville much longer.

I had a taste for river scenery. Every night, when I went for the mail, I used to see the steamboat on the river; and I often thought I should be "made" if I could make a trip in her. Ever since my brother wrote that he should take us down to New Orleans in the fall, I had looked forward with intense joy to the voyage down the river. In a smaller way my raft had afforded me a great deal of pleasure on the waters of the swamp, though the swift current did not permit me to embark on the stream.

Perhaps the decided course of Sim Gwynn in leaving his disagreeable situation had some influence upon my reflections. I had often thought of doing the same thing myself, and only my poor sister had prevented me from acting upon the suggestion. I had some money now. Why could I not go, and take her with me? But I had not enough to pay our fares to New Orleans, and there was no other place to which I could go. Besides, Captain Fishley would not let us go. If we went by any public conveyance, he could easily stop us.

"I have it!" I exclaimed, in a tone so loud that Sim was disturbed in his interesting occupation.

He started from his seat, and looked at me, with his mouth filled with food, his jaws suspending their pleasing occupation.

"Did you speak to me, Buck?" he called.

"No," I replied, walking towards him.

I looked at him, and realized that he was beginning to weary of his task. Doubtless he felt it to be a duty to eat all he could; but he had already disposed of the major part of what I had brought him, and was still struggling manfully with the balance.

"I heard you say, 'I have it,'" added Sim, jumbling the words through the food in his mouth.

"Well, I have it."

"So have I. That's the best meal of victuals I've had for a year. I'm sorry I can't eat no more."

"You will get hungry again."

"Shall I keep the rest of it?" he asked.

"Certainly; and when that is gone, I will bring you some more."

"Thank you, Buck. I knowed you'd help me, and that's what I wanted to see you for."

"I think I heard you say that before. Now, Sim, what are you going to do?"

"I don't know," he replied, blankly.

"You have left Barkspear's. Are you going back again?"

"I don't know. That's what I wanted to see you for."

"Haven't you any idea what you intend to do?"

"Not the leastest grain in the world. That's what I wanted to see you for, you see."

"But you wish to do something."

"I don't care. If I get enough to eat, it don't make no difference to me. I shan't get much to eat if I go back to Barkspear's."

This seemed to be the great question with him. He was willing to work hard for enough to eat. He was not a dandy, and the clothes question did not trouble him. It was only terrible to be hungry.

"Sim, I'm going to run away myself," said I.

"What, from Fishley's?" he demanded, opening his eyes.

"Yes, from Fishley's."

"Don't they give you enough to eat?"

"Plenty."

"What do you want to run away for, then?" asked he; and, if the provision question was all right, he did not think there ought to be trouble about any other matter.

"They don't use me well, and they don't use my sister well."

"But they give you enough to eat."

"I would rather be starved than treated like a dog. My brother Clarence is going to take us away in the fall; but I don't think I can stand it till that time."

I took off my coat, and showed him one of the wales of the cowhide which my tyrants had left upon my arm.

"But they give you all you want to eat," he replied, pulling away the rags from his shoulder, and exhibiting some marks like my own. "I don't mind them things much if they will only let me have something to eat."

Sim was a puzzle to me. He was all stomach. Blows were nothing; food was everything.

"Where have you been since yesterday?" I asked.

"Laying round, looking for something to eat."

"Sim, we must build a raft," I added.

"What for?" he inquired, opening his eyes, as he always did when his muddy brain seized an idea.

"To run away on. Do you see those logs and boards?"

"I see them."

"Well, Sim, we can build a big raft, with a house on it,—a place to live in,—where we can cook, and sleep, and eat."

"Eat!" exclaimed he, opening his mouth wide enough to take in a good-sized leg of bacon.

"Of course, if we live on the raft, we must have something to eat."

"Can we get enough?" he asked, incredulously.

"You shall have all you want."

"Goody!" shouted he.

"You must keep still about it, and not say a word to any one."

"I don't see nobody. I have to keep out of sight, or Barkspear will catch me. I'm bound to him. I shan't tell nobody."

"In a few days we will have the house ready for you to live in; and I will bring you all you need to eat."

"That's all I want."

"You can work on the raft, and I will help you all I can."

"I will work from daylight till dark, if I only get something to eat."

I pushed the raft over to the pile of lumber. I was quite excited as soon as the idea had taken full possession of my mind. I was not satisfied that the plan of leaving Torrentville with Flora, on a raft, was practicable; but I could have the fun of planning and building it; and really this was all I expected to do. If worse came to worst, I could get away from the town with my sister better by the way of the swamp than by the road. I explained to Sim more clearly what I intended to do, and how to construct the raft. He was even more enthusiastic than I was, for the scheme would enable him to help me, and thus pay for the provisions he consumed. He wanted to go to work at once; but nothing could be done without an axe, some nails, and other articles which I intended to procure.

I left Sim with the promise to see him again in the afternoon, and returned to the house. I was not attending school at all at this time, as the winter term had closed, and the summer one had not commenced, and I had nothing to do but work about the place. I went into the house, and talked with Flora. I told her what had happened—how I had been whipped by both father and son. She cried, and begged me not to disobey them any more.

"If they treat me decently, I will do all they tell me, Flora," I replied; "but I will not be trodden upon."

The conversation was interrupted by the arrival of the wagon, and I went out, in order that I might not be "tackled" before my sister. Captain Fishley gave me an ugly look; but I knew he would not say anything before his brother, and he did not. He told me I *might* put the horse up, and I did so. But I felt that the day of settlement would come as soon as the squire departed.

At dinner-time I was sometimes required to stay in the store, and I was directed to do so on this day. I selected a couple of stout clothes-lines, a shingling hatchet, and put up two pounds of ten-penny nails. I wrote down the articles on a piece of paper, and carried it, with the five-dollar bill taken from my roll, to the captain. He gave me the change, without knowing who the customer was, and I concealed the articles in the barn. When I had eaten my dinner, and taken care of Darky and the pigs, I started for the swamp again, with the goods I had bought.

CHAPTER XI.

BUILDING THE RAFT.

I FOUND Sim Gwynn at our landing-place on the verge of the swamp, which was a safe spot for him, as he could retreat, at the approach of a pursuer, where no one could follow him without a boat. On the raft lay a sharp axe, which assured me he had not remained in the swamp all the time during my absence.

"Where did you get that axe, Sim?" I asked, disturbed by an unpleasant fear that he had been disregarding the rights of property.

"I got it up to Barkspear's," replied he, laughing, as though he had done a clever thing.

"Then you must carry it back again, Sim. I won't have any stealing done!" I added, sharply.

"Hookie! You don't think I'd steal—do you, Buck Bradford?"

"Didn't you take that axe from Barkspear's?"

"Yes, I did; but that's my axe, you see; and that makes all the difference in the world. That axe was gin to me by Squire Mosely. His best cow got out, and came down into this swamp. She got mired in the mud, and couldn't get out. I dug her out for him, and took her home. Squire Mosely wanted to do something for me, and asked me what he should give me. I was going to say something to eat; but I felt kinder 'shamed. I was cuttin' wood for the fire, when he come over, with an old blunt axe, the only one Barkspear would let me use. So I told him I'd like a good axe, because I couldn't think of anything else I wanted. He gin me the best axe he could find in town. I used it when Barkspear wan't round; but I kept it hid away in the barn. I went up and got it after you left."

"All right, Sim; I don't want to have anything done that isn't right."

"What you goin' to do with them ropes, Buck?" he asked, as I threw the clothes-lines upon the raft.

"We want them to haul the logs out with."

Sim was in high spirits, and I concluded that he had filled himself again from the provisions I brought. I was confident that he would be satisfied as long as the rations were supplied. We poled the raft over to the branch of the creek; and, as I had the plan of the structure we were to build in my mind, we lost no time in commencing the work.

"I don't know what you're goin' to do, Buck," said Sim, as he picked up his axe; "but I can chop as well as the best on 'em. If you'll tell me what to do, I'll go into it like a hund'ed of bricks."

"You won't need your axe yet," I replied, assured there would be no difference of opinion in regard to the manner of constructing the raft, for my companion had few ideas of his own. "We must build the raft on the stream."

I selected two logs from the pile, thirty feet in length, attached one of the lines to each of them, and hauled them out of the pile of lumber, though not till after we had secured the boards, slabs, and other smaller pieces. We placed them side by side over the deep water. I then nailed each end of a couple of slabs to the inner log, at the two extremities of it. We next rolled the outer log away from the other until the two were ten feet apart, and the other end of the slab was nailed to it, thus forming the shape of the raft—thirty feet long, and ten feet wide.

"Now, Sim, we want another log thirty feet long," I continued, when the work was laid out.

"I see it," replied Sim; and, in his eagerness to be useful, I was fearful he would tumble into the river, for he was rather clumsy in his movements.

I cut one of the lines in two, and carefully secured the frame to the trees on shore, using the other line to float the logs down to the structure. There was only one other stick in the heap that was thirty feet in length, and we pushed this under the cross slabs, and nailed it half way between the two. For the rest of the groundwork of the raft we were obliged to use shorter sticks; but we made a solid platform of large logs.

"Now, Sim, bring on your slabs, ten feet long," said I, as I took my hatchet and nails.

"I'll fetch 'em as fast as you can nail 'em on," replied my willing assistant.

"Take this pole as a measure, and cut them off the right length. You can try your axe now," I added, throwing him a stick I had cut the width of the raft.

He kept me well supplied with materials, until I had covered the logs with slabs, nailing them down to each stick. By this time I had used up all my nails, and it was nearly the supper hour. I did not like to leave the work in which I was so much interested, but I had to go for the mail; and I wished to do so on the present occasion, in order to make some purchases in Riverport for the enterprise.

"I must go now, Sim," I said to my fellow-laborer.

"Hookie! You ain't a-goin' to stop work so soon—are you?" demanded he, with an aggrieved look.

"I must."

"But I want to do something more."

"You may cut up those small logs into pieces ten feet in length. They are to be placed crosswise on the raft, to keep us well up out of the water."

"I'll do it; and I'll have 'em all ready when you come down in the morning."

"Where are you going to sleep to-night, Sim?" I asked.

"I don't know—in somebody's barn," replied he with a grin, which made me feel that his lodging did not disturb him.

"You can sleep in our barn, if you like. No one goes into it very often, except myself."

"Thank ye, Buck. I always knowed you'd help me, and that was what I wanted to see you for."

"Have you anything left for supper?"

"Plenty, Buck. I couldn't eat all you gave me this forenoon."

"I will bring you a good supply in the morning."

I left him, and hastened back to the house. My tyrants had been so busy in entertaining their distinguished guest that they probably had not thought of me. The squire was in the parlor with Mrs. Fishley, who was as lovely as a summer day. She had company, and I was safe enough as long as the senator remained. My woes would come as soon as he departed; but I hoped to have the raft ready for a movement by that time.

Supper was not on the table, and I went into the store to see if the mail was ready. Mr. Barkspear was there, engaged in telling Captain Fishley that his good-for-nothing "help" had run away and left him.

"Hev you seen anything of Sim Gwynn?" said Mr. Barkspear, turning to me as I entered the store.

That was a hard question, and I decided not to pay any attention to it. I asked Ham if the mail was ready to go, and was hastening out to the barn to harness Darky, when Captain Fishley called me back.

"Are you deaf, Buck?" demanded he, sharply, and with that ugly look he had worn since our troubles began.

"Not much," I replied.

"Mr. Barkspear asked you if you had seen Sim Gwynn. Why don't you answer him?"

"I would rather not answer him," I replied; for, whatever other faults I had, I felt above lying and stealing.

"That means, I s'pose, that you have seen him," added Barkspear, in that peculiar whining tone which always indicates a mean, stingy man.

I made no reply, for I had no idea of betraying Sim, on the one hand, or of lying, on the other.

"Why don't you speak, Buck?" growled the captain.

"I have seen him, and he has run away. That's all I have to say about it."

"I didn't think your boy would try to kiver him up. Sim hadn't any business to run away, jest when he was gittin' big enough to be some help to me about the farm."

"I would have run away if I had been in his place," I ventured to remark, perhaps foolishly, for I could not bear to see Barkspear assuming to be an injured man, when his own meanness had driven poor Sim from his home.

"I allus took care on him, and sent him to school every winter, when there warn't much to do; and it's shameful for him to treat me so. He hain't got no gratitude in him."

"Did you have any trouble with him?" asked the captain.

"Well, we did hev a little yesterday mornin'. He stole some things out of the house, and I licked him for't," replied Barkspear, rather sheepishly.

"He ought to be licked if he stole," said Captain Fishley, glancing sternly at me; "or if he didn't behave himself, and be respectful to his employers."

"What did he steal, Mr. Barkspear?" I asked, indignantly.

"Well, he stole some things out of the buttery."

"Yes, sir! That's just what he stole—something to eat! He didn't have breakfast enough to keep his stomach from grumbling, and he stole a piece of boiled pork and some cold potatoes."

"That boy eats more'n enough for four men!" exclaimed Barkspear, in disgust.

"No matter if he does; he ought not to be starved. In this house we have enough to eat, and that which is first rate too. When Sim told me he didn't get enough to eat, I pitied him, for I'm not used to such things."

Captain Fishley almost smiled at this "first-rate notice" of the fare at his house; and my judicious commendation saved me any more hard questions from him.

"When boys are growing, they feed pretty strong," added the captain, now entirely non-committal.

"Sim was half starved, and I gave him some of the good things from our buttery; and I don't think anybody here will say I stole them. They don't call it stealing when any one takes something to eat, either for himself or to give to some one that's hungry."

Captain Fishley looked benevolent and magnanimous, but he did not say anything. He took credit to himself for the state of things I explained.

"Sim has run away, and if you want to know where he has gone, you must ask some one besides me," I added.

"There! that will do," interposed the captain, sternly. "You may go and harness the horse."

While I was hitching Darky to the post, I saw Barkspear leave the store, and I do not think he obtained much sympathy from Captain Fishley. I wish I could have spoken as highly of the Christian love and kindness of his house as I had of its hospitality and good fare. We had an extra nice supper that evening, out of respect to the distinguished guest. Everything was pleasant at the table, and Mrs. Fishley seemed to be the loveliest woman in the world. I am afraid there are a great many families that appear better before company than at other times.

When I was getting into the wagon to go to Riverport with the mail, Squire Fishley presented himself, and said he would ride a little way with me, and walk back. He seated himself by my side, and I drove off. I was glad he was only going a short distance, for his presence would have interfered with my operations in procuring supplies for the raft. But I was glad to see him alone, for I wished to ask him whether the whole forty-six dollars he had given me was intended for me. If it was a mistake, I did not desire to take advantage of it, though the loss of the money would defeat my enterprise with the raft.

CHAPTER XII.

SQUIRE FISHLEY MAKES IT RIGHT.

"DID you know how much money you gave me, Squire Fishley?" I asked of my distinguished companion, as I drove over the bridge.

"No, I did not; and I don't wonder that you ask, Buck," he replied, very solemnly.

"You gave me forty-six dollars, sir."

"Forty-six," he added, taking out his large pocket-book.

He did not seem to be at all astonished at the magnitude of the sum, and I wondered what he was going to do. Much as I dreaded the loss of the money, I was satisfied that he had made a mistake, and I felt that it would not be honest for me to keep it without informing him. Of course I expected to be commended for my honesty in refusing to take advantage of a drunken man's mistake; but he did not say a word, only fumbled over the thick pile of bank notes in his pocket-book, for the purpose, I judged, of ascertaining whether he had lost any or not. To my astonishment, however, he took two bills from the pile, and handed them to me.

"What's that for?" I asked, involuntarily taking the bills.

"I meant to give you more," said he.

"More!" I exclaimed.

"I didn't know what I was about very well last night," he added, with a groan which expressed the anguish he felt for his error. "I ought to have given you a hundred."

"Why, no, sir! I don't ask anything," I replied, confounded by his words.

"You don't understand it as well as I do," said he, shaking his head, and bestowing a mournful look upon me.

"But I can't take a hundred dollars, sir."

"Yes, you can, and you must. I shall not feel right about it if you don't. It ought to be a thousand; but I shall make it up to you some time."

"Why, Squire Fishley, if you had given me a couple of dollars, I should have thought you had treated me very handsomely," I protested.

"You saved my life."

"I don't know as I did."

"But you did more than that for me. I was intoxicated; I cannot deny it. I fell into the river in that state. If I had been found drowned, the cause of my death would have been rum!" he added, with a shudder. "I have always been classed with the moderate drinkers, though sometimes I don't taste of liquor for a week. Rather to oblige my friends than to gratify my own taste, I drank with them till I was in the state you saw me. I was drunk. What a scandal to my family, to my position, to my church! If it could have been said the Hon. Moses Fishley was drowned in consequence of getting intoxicated, I should not have slept in peace in my grave. You saved my life; and I am sure no one knew me, so that I hope to save my reputation. It has been a terrible lesson to me, and with God's forgiveness for the past, and his help for the future, I will never drink another drop of wine or liquor."

"I am sorry it happened, sir; but I am willing to do all I can for you without any money," I interposed.

"My gratitude, if nothing else, compels me to give you what I have given; and I hope you never will mention the matter."

"Never, sir!"

"I know that I deserve the humiliation of an exposure," continued the squire, in a very mournful tone; "but I feel that the facts would injure the cause of truth and religion more than they would injure me. My brother used to think I was a hypocrite because I attended to the concerns of the soul. I don't know that he has thought so since I went into the Senate. He used to laugh at me for going to the prayer meetings; and I don't know what he would say if he should learn that I got drunk and fell into the river."

"He will never find it out from me, sir; but I don't want all this money."

"Keep it; but I trust you will not spend it foolishly, nor let my brother know that you have it."

"I will do neither. Captain Fishley and I don't get along well enough together for me to say anything to him."

"Why, what's the matter?"

I told my story; for I felt that if the senator could trust me, I could trust him. I did not say anything about my half-formed intention to run away. The squire was very sorry there was any trouble; but, as it was a family matter, he did not like to say much about it, though he promised to do all he could for me.

"I think I won't go any farther, Buck," said he. "I suppose you will despise me, for you know me better than any other person."

"I'm sure I don't despise you."

"I'm confident my misfortune—if it can be called by that name—is all for the best. When I go home, I shall come out for temperance, and I think this journey will do me good."

I thought it must be very mortifying for him to talk to me in that way; but he was sincerely penitent, and I am sure he was a better Christian than ever before. He was a truer man than his brother in every respect, and I should have had a high regard for him, even if he had not given me a hundred dollars.

I had money enough now to pay my own and my sister's passage to New Orleans in a steamboat; but I was so fascinated with the raft that I could not think of abandoning it. I was going to build a house upon it; and my fancy pictured its interior, and the pleasure we might enjoy in it, floating down the river. It was a very brilliant ideal which I had made up in connection with the new craft.

In due time I reached Riverport, and obtained the mail-bag. At the post-office, I happened to meet the landlord of the hotel, who wanted to know how Squire Fishley was. I told him he was quite well.

"They say there was a man drowned in the river last night," he added. "I'm glad to hear from Squire Fishley."

"It wasn't the squire," I replied. "He went home with me."

"It was somebody else then; but nobody seems to know who it was."

I did not enlighten him. In the Riverport Standard there was an item in regard to the accident, which stated that "an elderly gentleman, under the influence of liquor, had fallen from the gang-plank of the steamer into the river," and that "a young man had attempted to save him; but, as neither of them had been heard from, it was supposed that both were drowned. But it was possible they had been saved, and had continued on their journey in that or some other steamer." I learned that a great deal had been said about the affair in the town, and I never heard that any satisfactory solution of the mystery was obtained. The squire was safe, and that was all I cared for.

At a store where I was not known I purchased ten pounds of nails, and such other articles of hardware as would be needed in carrying on the work upon the raft. The method of supplying Sim with provisions was a more difficult problem; but, at a restaurant near the steamboat landing, I bought a boiled ham, which I thought would keep my hungry assistant alive for several days. I also purchased a keg of crackers, half a cheese, a couple of loaves of soft bread, and a basket to carry them in. I was rich, and did not mind the expense.

When I arrived home, I took the basket and the hardware to the back side of the barn; but before I went to bed I saw Sim, and told him where they were. Before I made my appearance in the morning he had carried them away to the swamp. Everything had worked successfully thus far. Sim was in no danger of starving, and I was relieved of the necessity of feeding him from the buttery of the house.

I gave Squire Fishley a copy of the Standard, and pointed out to him the paragraph in relation to the "elderly gentleman under the influence of liquor." He turned pale and trembled as he read it; but I assured him he was perfectly safe, and that no one but myself was in possession of his secret.

After breakfast, when I had finished my regular "chores," I hastened to the swamp to work on the raft. I cannot describe the satisfaction which this labor, and the thinking of it, afforded me. It was fully equal to a trip down the river in a steamboat. Day after day, and night after night, in my trips to Riverport, and in my bed, I anticipated the voyage down the stream, and the pleasure of keeping house in our mansion on the raft, with Flora and Sim.

After three days' hard work, we had the body of the raft completed. We had covered the long logs with short ones, and on the upper tier laid a flooring of slabs, which were more plentiful than boards, as they were thrown away by the saw-mills above. The platform was more than a foot above the surface of the water, and I was confident that it would carry us high and dry.

It only remained to build the house—the most pleasing because it was the most difficult part of the job. This structure was to be eighteen feet long and six feet wide, placed in the middle of the platform. I put together two frames of the requisite size, forming the sills and plates of the building, and boarded them up and down, leaving three windows on each side, and a door at the rear end. I made the rafters of slabs, with the round side down.

On the fifth day, so enthusiastically had we labored, I expected to complete the outside of the house, so that Sim could sleep in it. I was putting on the last of the roof boards, which lapped over so as to shed the rain, when an unfortunate circumstance occurred to delay the work. My bow-legged friend and fellow-laborer was the most willing boy in the world. He was quite skilful in the use of the axe; but he was very awkward in his movements, and did not always work to the best advantage.

Towards the last of the work, we had come short of boards, and I was thinking of going to the saw-mills, seven miles up the stream, to buy a few to complete the work. But there was a heavy rain in the night, which raised the creek, and brought down quite a number of them. I had swung a boom out so as to catch them. Sim had just hauled one of these, soaked with water, out of the river. While he was raising the end to hand it up to me, on the roof, his feet slipped, and he went into the stream with a "chug," like a frog.

Sim could not swim, and he began to flop about in the wildest and most unreasonable manner. I threw him a board, but he did not seem to have sense enough to grasp it. I saw that he would be drowned in a moment more, unless he received more efficient help. I was fearfully alarmed for his safety; and, though I could swim like a fish, I doubted my ability to handle such a clumsy fellow in the water.

SIM GWYNN'S MISHAP.

Kicking off my shoes, I dived after him from the roof of the house; for he had gone down, and I was not sure that he would come up again. I could not help thinking that this accident had ruined my enterprise. Though it seemed to be a long time to me, and doubtless a much longer time to him, he had not been in the water more than three seconds when I dived after him.

I did not find him under the water; but, when I rose to the surface, I saw him a rod or more below me, floundering about like a crazy alligator.

CHAPTER XIII.

NEAR UNTO DEATH.

ALTHOUGH I was abundantly able to take care of myself in the water, and even to do a little more than that, I was really afraid to approach Sim Gwynn, he struggled so violently. I was satisfied, if I did so, that he would swamp me as well as himself. We were both floating down the stream with the current, and all the chances seemed to be against us.

Sim had struggled till his strength was in a measure wasted. I saw that he was going down again, and though I feared it would cost me my own life, I decided to grapple with him. A couple of strokes with my arms brought me to him, and I seized him by the collar. The moment he was conscious of the presence of something near him, he began to struggle more violently than ever. He threw his arms tight around my body, and hugged me in what I thought would be the death-gripe.

Vainly I tried to shake him off. The more I labored, the closer he clung to me, as if fearful that I should escape his grasp. I believed that my last moment had come. I gave myself up in despair, and thought of Flora—what would become of her. I asked God to forgive all my sins—which seemed like a mountain to me in that awful moment.

I rested but an instant while these thoughts rushed through my brain. I felt myself going down. It was useless to do so, I felt; but I could not help making one more struggle for the boon of life. It would have been useless if a kind Providence had not come to my aid, for my strength was nearly exhausted, and I was utterly inadequate to the task of bearing up the heavy burden of my companion.

My head struck against a log, one end of which had grounded on the shore, while the other projected out over the deep water of the stream. I clutched it, threw my arms around it, and hugged it as though it was the dearest friend on earth. I threw myself across it, so as to bring Sim's head out of the water, and waited to recover my wasted breath. Our united weight on the end of the log detached it from the shore, and we were again floating down the stream. I clung to my support; and such a sweet rest as that was I had never before known. The life seemed to come back to me, and every breath of air I drew in was a fountain of strength to my frame.

Still Sim clung to me, and appeared not to know that there was anything else to sustain him. As my powers came back to me, I drew myself farther up on the log, and tried to release my body from the gripe of my senseless companion.

"Sim!" I shouted.

He did not answer me. Was he dead? I trembled at the thought.

"Sim!" I cried again, louder than before.

"Ugh!" said he, with a shudder that thrilled my frame.

He was not dead, or even wholly unconscious. With one arm hugging the log, I tried with the other to release myself from his bearish gripe.

"Let go of me, Sim!" I screamed to him.

But he would not, or could not. After a desperate effort, I succeeded in throwing one of my legs over the log; and, thus supported, I found myself better able to work efficiently. With a mighty struggle, I shook him off, and he would have gone to the bottom if I had not seized his hand as he threw it up. I placed his arm on the log, and he grappled with it as though it had been a monster threatening his destruction.

After pausing a moment to rest, I pulled him farther up on the log. Then, for the first time, I felt safe. The battle had been fought, and won. I believed Sim had lost his senses. He was stupefied, rather than deprived of any actual power. It was the terror rather than any real injury which overcame him. I permitted him to remain quiet for a moment, to recover his breath.

"Sim!" said I, when he began to look around him, and show some signs of returning reason.

"Ugh! That's what I wanted to see you for, Buck," gasped he.

I could not laugh, though his wild stare and incoherent words were ludicrous.

"You are safe now, Sim," I added.

"I'm dead—drownded."

"No, you are not. You are safe."

"No! Am I? Hookie!"

I had placed myself astride the log, and was now in a comfortable position. I moved up to him, when I found it was safe to approach him, and assisted him into an easier posture. Gradually I restored him to his former self, and finally assured him that he was still in the land of the living, where he might remain if he would only be reasonable.

"Where are we going to?" he asked.

"Down the river."

"Down to New Orleans?"

"Not yet, if you will behave like a man. Have a little pluck, Sim."

"I dassent!" replied he, with a shake of his frame.

"Now hold on tight! I'm going to try to get ashore," I called to him, as I saw that the current would carry us under the overhanging branch of a tree, which I could reach by making a strong effort.

"Don't leave me, Buck!" pleaded he, in his terror.

"I won't leave you. Cling to the log," I replied, as I jumped up, and succeeded in grasping the branch of the tree.

I pulled it down till I got hold of a part strong enough to check the progress of the log; but the current was so swift that I was nearly dragged from it. By twining my legs around the log, I held on till its momentum was overcome; and then I had no difficulty in drawing it in till the end touched the shore. After much persuasion I induced Sim to work himself along the stick till he reached the dry land; for we had passed beyond the greatest depression in the swamp, where the stream did not cover the banks.

Eagerly he passed from the log to the bank, and actually danced with joy when he found himself once more on the solid earth.

"Hookie! Hookie!" shouted he, opening his mouth from ear to ear, while his fat face lighted up with an expression of delight, like a baby with a new rattle.

"Are you going to let me go down stream, Sim?" I called to him, reproachfully, for he seemed to have more regard for his own safety than for mine.

"What shall I do?" he asked, blankly; and he appeared to have an idea that I could not possibly need any assistance from him.

"Catch hold of the end of the log, and haul it up so that I can get ashore. If I let go the branch, the log will go down stream again."

Sim lifted the log, and hauled it far out of the water. He was as strong as an ox now, though he had been as weak as an infant a few moments before. I crawled up the stick, and went ashore. The moment I was fairly on the land, Sim threw his arms around my neck, and hugged me as though I had been his baby, blubbering in incoherent terms his gratitude and love.

"Hold on, Sim! You have hugged me enough for one day," said I, shaking him off.

"Hurrah! Hurrah!" shouted he.

"Silence, Sim," I added.

I threw myself on my knees, dripping with water as I was.

"O Lord God, I thank thee for saving my life, and for saving Sim's life. In my heart I thank thee, O Lord. May it be a good lesson to him and me. May we both try to be better boys, and obey thy holy law as we have never done before."

I had never prayed before in my life, but I could not help it then. I felt that God had saved my life, and that I could not be so wicked as not to pray to him then. My heart was full of gratitude, and I felt the better for speaking it.

I opened my eyes, and saw Sim kneeling before me, very reverently, and I realized that he was as sincere as I was. He was not satisfied with hearing. He uttered a prayer himself, using nearly my own words. He finished, and both of us were silent for several minutes. However long I may live, I shall never forget the agony of that fearful moment, when, with Sim clinging to me, I felt myself going down, never to come up; never to see the light of the blessed sun again; never more to look into the eyes of my loving sister. The influence of that thrilling incident will go with me to the end of my days, and I am sure it has made me a better man.

We walked through the swamp to the open prairie beyond, where the sun shone brightly. We took off our clothes, and wrung them out, and then lay in the sunshine to dry them. We talked of the event of the afternoon, and Sim, in his bungling speech, poured forth his gratitude to me for saving his life. I staid there till it was time for me to go back to the house. My clothes were still wet, and I crept through the back entry up to my chamber and changed them. Squire Fishley was going home that day, and was to ride down to Riverport with me.

I was sorry he was going, for during his visit our house seemed to be a paradise. Mrs. Fishley was all smiles, and never spoke a cross word, never snarled at Flora or at me. If the squire had been a steady boarder at his brother's, I should have been content to cut my raft adrift, and let it go down the river without me. He was going home, and there would be a storm as soon as he departed.

During the week of the senator's stay, not a word was said about Miss Larrabee's letter; and Ham appeared about the same as usual. I observed his movements with interest and curiosity. Sometimes I thought he was more troubled than was his habit. After the thrashing his father had given me, he seemed to be satisfied that I had been "paid off," and he was tolerably civil to me, though I concluded that he did not wish to have any more difficulty during the visit of the distinguished guest.

After supper, with my passenger, I drove down to Riverport. On the way he talked very kindly to me, and gave me much good advice. He counselled me to "seek the Lord," who would give me strength to bear all my troubles. He told me he had spoken to his brother about me, but he was afraid he had done more harm than good, for the captain did not seem to like it that I had said anything to the guest about my ill usage.

I bade him good by at the hotel, where he was to spend the night; and we parted the best of friends, with a promise on his part to do something for me in the future. After changing the mail-bags at the post-office, I went to several stores, and picked up various articles to furnish the house on the raft, including a small second-hand cook-stove, with eight feet of pipe, for which I paid four dollars, and a few dishes and some table ware.

I succeeded in placing these things in the wheelbarrow, back of the barn, without detection. Early in the morning Sim wheeled them down to the swamp. When I joined him after breakfast, I found he had waded through the water to the branch, and brought up the small raft, upon which he had loaded the stove and other articles. Before noon that day, the outside of the house was done, and the cook-stove put up. I went home to dinner as usual, that my absence might not be noticed.

"Where have you been all the forenoon?" demanded Captain Fishley, in the most uncompromising of tones.

The storm was brewing.

CHAPTER XIV.

WHO ROBBED THE MAIL.

"WHERE on airth have you been?" said Mrs. Fishley, chiming in with her husband; and if I had not realized before, I did now, that the squire had actually gone home.

"I haven't been a great ways," I replied.

As the fact of my absence, rather than where I had been, was the great grievance with my tyrants, I concluded not to tell them in what precise locality I had spent the forenoon. The old order of things was fully restored. It was snap, snarl, and growl. But I soon learned that there was something more than this. Captain Fishley and Ham both looked glum and savage; but they ate their dinner in silence.

"Buck, I want you," said the captain, in a very ugly tone, as I was going to the barn after dinner. "Come into the store."

I followed him into the shop. He sat down behind the post-office counter, looked at me sternly, and then gazed at the floor.

"Where have you been to-day?" said he, after his gaze had vibrated for some time between me and the floor.

"I haven't been far."

"Buck, have you got any money?" he added, sharply, and putting the question as a home thrust at me.

"Yes, sir, I have," I replied, startled by the inquiry; for it was evident to me now that the storm was coming in the shape of a tempest.

"How much have you got?"

"I haven't got any of your money," I answered.

If Ham could rob the mail, it would not be a very hard step for him to take to rob his father's pocket-book; and I began to think he had done so, charging the crime upon me.

"I didn't say you had got any of my money," added Captain Fishley. "I asked you how much you had."

"What do you want to know for?"

"No matter what I want to know for. Why don't you answer me?"

"Because I don't choose to answer you," I replied, saucily.

I felt innocent, and I could not tell him anything about my money without exposing his brother. He made a movement towards me, and I thought he was going to seize me by the collar. I jumped over the counter, for I had all my money in my pocket, and I did not care about being searched.

"Come back here!" said he, savagely.

"I am just as well here."

"Will you tell me how much money you have got, or shall I send for the constable?" he continued.

"You may send for the constable, if you like; but I haven't any money that belongs to you, or anybody but myself."

"Yes, you have! You have been robbing the mail!" retorted my tyrant, fiercely.

Robbing the mail! I saw through the mill-stone. The postmaster had heard from Miss Larrabee, or her brother, in regard to the missing letter, and I was accused of purloining it! No doubt Captain Fishley thought I was the robber. Probably Ham had charged the crime upon me, and his father was willing to believe him.

"I have not robbed the mail," I replied, smartly.

"Yes, you did; and I can prove it. You had better own it, and give back the money."

"I didn't take the money."

"What's the use to deny it, Buck?" said he, more mildly. "If you will own it, and give back the money, I will try and make it as easy as I can for you."

"I tell you I didn't take the money, and I won't own it when I didn't do it."

"Well, just as you like, Buck. If you won't give up the money, I shall have to hand you over to the constable, and see what he can do."

"You may hand me over to the constable as much as you please. Neither he nor anybody else can make me own up to what I didn't do."

"Why will you persist in saying you didn't do it?"

"Because I didn't do it."

"I can prove it."

"Let's see you prove it."

"You carry the mail to Riverport and back."

"I know it; but I don't have any key to the bag."

"You know where the key is," said he, earnestly. "This morning I had a letter from Miss Larrabee's brother, saying that he sent his sister forty dollars, which must have come on before she left."

"That don't prove that I took it," I interposed; for I wished to know what the trap was before I said anything about Ham.

"It proves that the letter came. I've been down to Riverport this forenoon, and seen the postmaster there. He says the name was an odd one to him, and he distinctly remembers seeing it when he sorted the mail. I haven't any doubt the letter came to this office."

"Nor I either," I replied, glancing at Ham, who had taken position by his father's side to hear what was said.

"What do you mean by that?" demanded Captain Fishley, puzzled by my remark.

"You haven't proved that I took the letter."

"It came here, but none of us saw it. The very night the mail containing that letter came in, you were seen counting money."

"Who saw me?" I asked.

"Ham saw you—didn't you, Ham?" replied the captain, appealing to his son.

"Yes, I did. After I came home from Crofton's, I put on my old rubbers, and went out to the barn after the lantern. I found Buck on the hay-loft, counting a roll of bank bills," answered Ham, glibly.

"How much was there?" asked the postmaster.

"I asked him how much he had, but he wouldn't tell me," replied Ham. "He said it was a little money that he had made on his own account."

"How did you make it, Buck?"

"I made it honestly, and I did not steal it," was the only safe answer I could give.

I confess that it must have looked very bad for me; but I could not expose Squire Fishley, and my lips were sealed.

"How much did there appear to be, Ham?" continued Captain Fishley; and I must do him the justice to say that he now appeared to be only anxious to elicit the truth.

"I don't know. I thought there were five or six bills. It was a good deal of money for him to have, anyhow. I didn't think much about it till since we found this letter was lost."

"Didn't you, Ham Fishley?" said I, looking him right in the eye. "*You* know very well that I didn't take that letter."

"I know it!" repeated he, trying to bluster; but I saw that it was hard work.

"Yes, you know it, if your father don't."

"I don't see who could have taken it, if he didn't," added Ham, turning to his father.

"Don't you, Ham?" I shouted, in my excitement.

"Of course he took it," said the postmaster. "He isn't willing to tell where he got that money, which he don't deny having."

"I can't tell where I got it, without injuring some one else; but I most solemnly declare that I did not steal it, nor take the letter."

"That's all in your eye," said Ham.

"It *was* all in my eye the night the mail was robbed," I replied. "I didn't do it; but I saw it done; and I know who did it, Ham Fishley."

"Humph! I shouldn't wonder if he meant to lay it to me, father!" added Ham.

"That's just what I mean to do. I saw Ham take the money out of the envelope, and then burn the letter."

"Well, that's a good one!" said Ham, laughing heartily; but his face was pale, and his laugh hollow.

Captain Fishley looked at his son earnestly. Perhaps he saw the unrealness of his mirth. Ham was extravagant in his demonstrations, and so far overdid the matter, that even his father must have been troubled with a suspicion that all was not right in relation to him.

"Buck Bradford, you have a large sum of money about you," said he. "Have you not?"

"No matter how much," I answered.

"You have forty dollars. Will you deny it?"

"I will neither own nor deny it. I have nothing to say about it."

"Ham saw you have five or six bills. Now, you must tell me where you got that money, or I shall believe you robbed the mail."

"I shall not tell you," I replied, firmly. "If it was right for me to do so, I would; but it isn't right, and I can't."

"That's rich!" sneered Ham. "If you want any better evidence than that, you will have to send to Texas after it. His trying to lay it to me is the best proof I want."

"Ham Fishley, you know that what I have said is true," I continued indignantly. "You know that you opened that mail-bag after you came home from Crofton's, put the money in your pocket, and burned the letter."

"Of course that's perfectly ridiculous," said Ham, angrily.

"I'm tired of this jaw," added Captain Fishley, in disgust. "Buck, come round here."

"I know what you want, and I think I won't do it," I replied, leaving the store.

"Ham, go over to Stevens's, and tell him I want to see him," said my tyrant, coming to the door.

Stevens was a constable. I was not anxious to see him. I went to the barn, and by a roundabout way reached the swamp. I need hardly say that I was in great excitement and alarm. The constable was to be put upon my track; but I was not at all afraid that he would find me in the swamp, which for nearly half a mile had three feet of water on the ground. He could not reach me at the raft without a boat.

I went to work upon the interior of the house, put up a partition to divide Flora's room from the rest of the space, and built a bunk in her apartment. I had already rigged a steering oar, and at one end of the raft I had set up a mast, on which I intended to spread a square-sail for use when the wind was favorable. I worked very hard all the afternoon, and kept Sim as busy as I was myself in sawing boards of the right length for the work.

The raft was in condition to go down the river, though it was not yet finished. I was ready to start that very night, if necessary. I was confident that I was to be persecuted, if not prosecuted, for robbing the mail. As long as I could not explain where I obtained the money which Ham had unfortunately seen, I was not able to clear myself of the suspicion. Before I left the swamp, I concealed all my money, but a few dollars, in the hollow of a tree.

I was not afraid of the constable. I determined to go back to the house, and trust to my wits for safety. I went into the kitchen as usual, where Captain Fishley and his wife were just sitting down to supper.

"Where have you been all the afternoon?" asked he, in a milder tone than I expected to hear him use.

"Keeping out of the way of the constable," I replied.

"I don't want to call the constable for you, but I shall if you don't give up the money," added Captain Fishley.

"I haven't got it. What I said about Ham was the truth."

"The wicked wretch!" gasped Mrs. Fishley. "Why don't you send for the constable?"

Poor Flora had heard the story about me, and she trembled with apprehension. How I pitied her!

"I will hand him over to Stevens to-morrow, if he don't give up the money before that time," added the captain.

I was not permitted to go after the mail that night. The postmaster went himself, and his wife accompanied him to "do some shopping."

CHAPTER XV.

THE DEPARTURE.

I HARNESSED the horse for Captain Fishley, and put the mail-bag in the wagon, as I was told to do. I could not help thinking that my tyrants were playing some deeper game than appeared upon the surface. They were certainly looking up evidence to enable them to convict me of robbing the mail. If the captain should happen to blunder into some of the stores in Riverport where I had made some extensive purchases, as I regarded them, he might wonder what I had done with a second-hand cooking-stove, about twenty pounds of nails, and other articles upon which boys do not usually set a high value; but the amount of money employed in the transaction would be of greater interest to him.

Captain Fishley drove off, and I went into the store. Ham was alone there, and the glance which he bestowed upon me was unusually ugly. I was uneasy and nervous. I knew I should never have any peace till I told where I had obtained the money in my possession; but Squire Fishley had specially interdicted my saying anything to his brother. It seemed to me just as though my chief tyrant had gone down to Riverport on purpose to find something which would condemn me. I had bought at least ten dollars' worth of goods at one store, and if he could prove that I had expended this sum of money, it would be enough to satisfy him that I had robbed the mail.

I felt that the storm was coming down upon me like a tempest. My tyrants were anxious to condemn me. Ham, in whom there was no sentiment of justice or magnanimity, would do his utmost to convict me, in order to save himself. It was plain enough to me, that without the testimony of Squire Fishley, I could not hope to escape. Ham was a villain; he knew that I had not stolen the money. I could not blame Captain Fishley and his wife for deeming me guilty; but I could not save myself at the expense of Squire Fishley. I had promised him faithfully, and he had handsomely rewarded me for my silence.

"You are bound to have a row with me, Buck Bradford," said Ham, as I sat in the store thinking of the perils of the situation.

"I think the boot's on the other leg," I replied.

"What do you mean by saying I robbed the mail then?"

"Well, what do you mean by saying I did it?" I retorted.

"You can't tell where you got that money I saw you have."

"No matter whether I can or not. You know, if nobody else does, that it didn't come out of that letter."

"What do you mean by that?"

"What's the use of talking, Ham Fishley?" I replied, impatiently. "Didn't you hear the dog howling that night when you broke open Miss Larrabee's letter, and put the money in your pocket? I did, and I went down stairs in my stocking feet to let him in. When I came to the store door, I saw what you were doing. I saw you set the letter afire, and throw it into the stove. Then you put the envelope in after it. But that didn't burn up, and I saved a piece of it in the morning when I made the fire."

"That's a pretty story!" exclaimed Ham; but I saw that he was pale, and that his lips quivered. "Do you expect any one to believe it?"

"I don't expect your father to believe it; but, if you want to fetch the constable, I think I can make him believe it."

"I went for the constable, but he was not in."

"Lucky for you!"

"You haven't told where you got that money."

"I don't mean to tell; but I think I can fetch some one to explain it, if the worst comes," I added.

It was useless to talk with him. My secret sealed my lips and tied my hands. I could do nothing, and it seemed like folly for me to stay and face my tyrants, who would enjoy my ruin. I could appeal to the senator to save me; but, if he did so, it would be at the expense of his own reputation, and he would not thank me for putting him in such an unpleasant position. If it had not been for Flora, I would have fled that instant. Though I had prepared the raft for her accommodation, I hardly expected she would be willing to go with me.

I went from the store into the kitchen, where I found the poor girl at the stove. She had been crying, and I had never before seen her look so sad and hopeless.

"What is the matter, dear Flora?" I asked, seating myself at her side.

"Nothing, Buckland."

"You have been crying, Flora."

"I couldn't help it."

"What made you cry?"

"I don't want to make trouble," she replied, the tears coming to her eyes again; "but I wish it was October, that we might leave this house. I'm sure Clarence does not know how much we suffer."

"Has Mrs. Fishley been abusing you again?"

She looked at me, and wiped away her tears before she answered.

"I did not mean to tell you of it, Buckland; but she did shake me again, and she hurt me very much," sobbed she.

"I'll tear her in pieces for it!" I cried, angrily; and my teeth ground together, and my fists involuntarily clinched.

"No, no, brother! Don't say anything about it," pleaded Flora. "Perhaps it was my fault; I contradicted her. She said you stole the money from the letter, and I persisted that you did not. O, Buckland, that was awful—to say you were a thief! I could not bear it."

"I am not a thief!"

"But have you some money?"

"I have."

"Where did you get it?" she asked, anxiously.

"I cannot tell them where I got it. I will tell you a little; but you must not breathe a word of it to any one."

"I will not, Buckland."

"I saved the life of a gentleman who had been drinking too much; and he gave me the money. He made me promise that I would not tell any one about it."

"Who was he?" asked she, excited by my story.

"I cannot tell even you who he was. He was very penitent, and wished me to save his character. Flora, it was Ham who robbed the mail. I saw him do it."

I told her what I had seen in the store the night the senator arrived, and that Ham accused me of the crime in order to save himself.

"You will be sent to prison, Buckland!" exclaimed she, in terror, as she threw her arm around my neck. "Ham hates you, and so do his father and mother."

"Dear Flora, if you will go with me, I will not stay another night with our tyrants. They abuse us both."

"Where will you go?"

"To New Orleans."

I will not pause to detail the arguments by which I convinced her that it was best for us to leave Torrentville at once. In the morning the constable would be sent for; and, while those who were left as my protectors were really my enemies, I could not hope to escape their malignity. This was the reasoning of a boy. Doubtless I was influenced by the fact that the raft was ready for use, and by a desire to embark upon a period of adventure.

"How can we go?" asked she; for I had said nothing to her about my craft yet.

"I have built a raft with a house upon it," I replied.

"A raft!"

"Yes; it is big enough to hold twenty men."

"But we can't go to New Orleans on a raft."

"Perhaps not; but when we get tired of it, we can take a steamboat and go the rest of the way. We shall have no tyrants to vex us," I added, with enthusiasm. "I have made a nice house for you, dear Flora."

"I will do anything you say, Buckland," said she, clasping her arms around my neck. "I cannot stay here."

"Then we must go this very night, before Captain Fishley and his wife return. The raft is in the swamp. Go and dress yourself in your warmest clothes, and put everything in a bundle which you wish to carry with you."

"Shall we stay on the raft night and day, Buckland?" she inquired, curiously; and her face already wore an expression of relief.

"Certainly, Flora. I have made a bunk in your room, and there is a stove in the house."

"Is the house furnished?"

"Not much," I replied. "We have some things."

"You know all the furniture in my room here belongs to us," she added.

I did know it, but I had not thought of it before. When we went from our own home to Captain Fishley's, Clarence had brought all the furniture from Flora's room. I decided to carry off as much as I could of it, including her bed, and the little rocking-chair in which she always sat. Flora went to her chamber to prepare for her departure, and I hastened to make my arrangements.

The die was cast! I was going immediately. Before the morning sun rose, Flora and I, borne by the swift current of the river, would be far away from Torrentville. My plans were all formed. Captain Fishley and his wife would not return before nine o'clock, and I had nearly three hours to convey Flora and her effects to the raft. There were no windows in the rear of the store, and I was not in much danger of being seen by Ham. I went to the barn to procure the wheelbarrow, and a little wagon I had made for Flora, in which I intended to draw her to the swamp.

"Buck!" shouted Ham, as I was bringing out these vehicles, "I want you."

I deemed it prudent not to have a fuss with him then, and I hastened to the store. In front of it I found the stable-keeper's best team. My elegant tyrant was doubtless going to take Miss Elsie Crofton out to ride, during the absence of his father.

"I want you to stay in the store till it's time to shut up," said Ham. "I haven't left any money where you can steal it."

"I shall not stay in the store," I replied, indignant at his gratuitous fling at me.

"Won't you?"

"No, I won't! I'm not going to put myself in position to be accused of anything else."

"I think you'd better do as I tell you."

"I don't think so. The old man will give you fits for leaving the store; and you know he wouldn't trust me there."

"The money is safe."

"That's all, Ham Fishley;" and I left the store.

I waited a little while to see what he would do. He locked the store, and drove off with the fine team. He knew his father would not be back till after it was time to close the shop. The coast was clear, and I lost not a moment in carrying out my plans. I took an armful of Flora's things, and went down to the verge of the swamp with them. I called Sim, and told him what I intended to do as we walked back to the house. Our operations were all carried on in the rear of the house, where none of the neighbors could see us; and I loaded down the wheelbarrow to its utmost capacity. But even then we could not carry everything, and I left several bundles behind the barn, where we could readily obtain them for a second load. I intended to take Bully with me, but I could not find him. He was in the habit of making journeys about the village, and he missed his destiny by being absent at this time.

It was after sundown when our little procession started for the swamp. I felt as though I was taking the great step of my lifetime, and winning the final triumph over my tyrants.

CHAPTER XVI.

DOWN THE RIVER.

FIRST steps are always full of interest, at least to those who take them; and, as I look back upon the eventful time when our little procession left the back of the barn, it looms up as the most exciting moment of my life, if I except the instant when I was struggling with Sim Gwynn in the water. I was leaving the only home I had known for years, and was going on a strange voyage down the river on a raft. I shall not soon forget the emotions which agitated me.

DOWN THE RIVER.

Sim led the way with the wheelbarrow piled high with Flora's bed, bundles of clothing, blankets, sheets, and comforters, while I brought up the rear, dragging Flora's wagon, in which she was seated. My poor sister was quite cheerful, and did not seem to be disturbed by any timidity.

"Hurry up, Sim!" I called to my file-leader. "We have no time to lose."

"Won't Captain Fishley come after us?" asked Flora, as Sim quickened his pace.

"He will if he knows where to come; but the swamp will be the last place in the world where any one would think of looking for us. Before morning we shall be miles away. Don't be alarmed, Flora."

"I am not alarmed. I feel ever so much better than I did when I thought of meeting Mrs. Fishley again. Do you think it is right for us to do this, Buckland?"

"Right! Of course it is. I don't know of any reason why we should stay with Captain Fishley and his wife, to be kicked and cuffed by them any longer."

Flora was thoughtful; but I knew she would not have come with me if she had believed it was wrong to do so. We were all silent till we reached the verge of the swamp, where the small raft lay. We unloaded the wheelbarrow, and Sim went back for the rest of the articles. I placed my sister's bed on the raft, and taking her in my arms, I laid her upon it, and covered her with blankets, that the night air might not injure her. I then pushed the raft over to the branch of the creek.

"Is that the raft?" exclaimed Flora, as I pointed it out to her.

"That's it; and I am sure you will be happier on board of it than at Fishley's."

"The house looks real nice! There is the stove-pipe. You have one glass window."

"Yes; that is in your room," I replied, as I ran the tender alongside the great raft.

I fastened it securely, and helped Flora on board. She was almost as much delighted with my handiwork as I had been myself. I conveyed her bed to her apartment, and placed it in the bunk. It was not a bad fit.

"Now, Flora, I must leave you, and go for the rest of the things. You can lie down in your bed, and I will cover you with blankets."

"I'm not cold. Shall you be gone long?" she asked.

"No."

"This is a very dismal place."

"You shall be on the broad river in the morning."

She lay down, and I left her to meet Sim at the landing-place. He had arrived before me, and we loaded all the rest of the goods on the raft.

"What shall I do with the wheelbarrow?" asked Sim.

"Take it up into the open field, where they can see it. It might lie in the swamp for a year before any one found it; and I don't mean to take a single thing from Fishley. I carried back the saw I borrowed, and bought a new one. I don't owe him anything now," I replied.

"I reckon he'll wonder where you and Miss Flora are, when he gets back," said Sim, with one of his broad grins.

"Let him wonder. I shall not charge him anything for wondering."

"I s'pose not," chuckled Sim, as he went off with the wheelbarrow.

While he was gone, I amused myself in picking up a quantity of dry wood on the high ground for the stove, which I placed upon the raft. As soon as Sim returned, we pushed off, and made our last trip through the swamp. When we arrived at the raft, I found Flora had got up, and was walking about the platform. She was so nervous she could not lie in bed. I placed her chair in the large room, closed the shutters, and made a fire in the stove. In a few minutes I had the pleasure of seeing her seated before the fire, seemingly comfortable and happy.

Sim and I transferred the articles, including Flora's wagon, from the small raft to the house on the large one. By this time it was quite dark, and I lighted my lantern. My first work was in Flora's room, where I made up the bed, and spread a rug on the floor. I drove nails into the walls to hang her clothes upon, and arranged her boxes on some shelves I had put up. The place looked very cosy to me, and Flora declared that it was ever so much nicer than she had expected. I had taken great pains with this part of the building, and carefully stopped every crack where the wind could blow through upon her, and the roof had already been tested in a heavy shower.

By nine o'clock, as nearly as I could guess the time, I had finished my sister's room; but, though it was past her bedtime, she was not willing to retire. I had hoped she would take to her bed at the usual hour, and relieve me of all anxiety about her, for I was afraid she would catch cold and be sick. But the excitement would not permit her to do so. The stove warmed both of the rooms, and we were in more danger from the want of ventilation than from the night air. She sat in her chair in her room, with Sim and me before her, talking over the matter.

"Why don't you start, Buckland?" she asked, when I had detailed more fully than before my plans.

"It is rather too early yet. You know the road to Riverport runs along the bank of the creek, and I don't wish anybody in these parts to see us," I replied.

"The sooner we start, the farther we shall get before morning," added Sim, who was as impatient as Flora.

"We shall be far enough off in the morning. How fast do you suppose the raft will go, Sim?"

"I dunno."

"It will go about as fast as the current without any help; and that is three or four miles an hour. We shall be at least twenty miles from here at five o'clock in the morning."

"But won't they miss us at the house, Buckland?" asked Flora.

"Certainly they will. Very likely they have missed us by this time."

"Suppose they should find us?"

"We should be no worse off than before. But there is not the remotest chance that they will find us. Do you think they would look in the swamp for you, Flora?"

She was satisfied, and we continued to discuss the future, until I judged that it was late enough to commence the voyage. I wished to be sure that Captain Fishley and his wife had returned from Riverport. The night was quite dark, and I had no fear that the raft would be seen; but even if it were, it was not a very uncommon thing for such a craft to go down the river.

I had made a crooked steering oar, and built a platform to stand upon, so that the helmsman could see over the house. I mounted this platform, and took hold of the end of the oar.

"Now cast off the forward fast, Sim!" I called to my deck hand.

"All clear," replied Sim, when he had drawn in the line, which had been passed round a tree so that it could be hauled in without going on shore.

"Now let go the other!"

Sim untied one of the ends of the rope, and was pulling it in, when I felt a consciousness that something was wrong, though I could not tell what. It flashed across my mind that I was making a blunder.

"Hold on, Sim!" I shouted, jumping down from the platform, and trying to catch the rope; but the end had gone ashore.

"What's the matter, Buck?" called Sim, apparently alarmed by my sudden movements.

"I have forgotten my money!" I exclaimed, as I leaped on the small raft which lay alongside.

I sprang for the tree to which the great raft was fastened, in order to secure the rope; but it was too late. The current started the raft, and dragged the rope off before I could catch hold of it. In the darkness and the night the craft went off without me.

"Don't leave me, Buck!" called Sim.

"Take the steering oar, and run her up to the shore!" I replied.

I had the small raft, and I could follow at pleasure, and join my companions; but if I pushed off, I could not return, for the branch of the creek was too deep for me to use the pole. I could not think of going without my money.

I saw Sim jump upon the platform, and work the steering oar vigorously, but with more power than skill. He succeeded in running her up to the bank.

"Now hold on to her!" I shouted. "I shall not be gone long!"

I pushed the raft to the tree where I had concealed the money; and, though I had some difficulty in finding it, I succeeded; still, three times as many minutes were wasted in the operation as I supposed would be necessary. With the roll of bills in my pocket-book, I pushed off again, and soon reached the stream. Launching out into the current, the raft was borne with its flow towards the creek.

I could not see the light on the raft where I had left it, only a few rods below the starting-point. My frail bark was not large enough to float easily on the rapid stream, and in spite of my best efforts, it would whirl round, for the pole in my hand had not blade enough to enable me to steer with it. In a few moments I reached the place where I had last seen the light through the window of Flora's room; but the raft was not there. It was not to be seen before me; but the stream made a bend a short distance below me.

The raft had probably broken loose, and Sim had been unable to stop it; but it was not like my fellow-voyager to let it go without yelling at the top of his lungs, and he had more voice than wits. Though all my hopes were in the ark I had built, and Flora, whom I loved more than life, was a passenger upon it, I was not alarmed. Sim would be able to run it up to the shore, and probably had done so beyond the bend.

I always had a habit of looking on the bright side of things, and was disposed never to despair; at least not till I had seen what was beyond the next bend in the stream of life. I was quite confident I should find the ark of my safety in a few moments more, and I did not even attempt to hurry the crazy float on which I travelled. I reached the bend, and strained my eyes to peer through the gloom, which hung deep and heavy over the swamp. The stream was straight for half a mile ahead of me, but no light gladdened my eyes.

I was startled, and even terrified, by the situation.

CHAPTER XVII.

NIGHT ON THE RIVER.

SIM GWYNN had a voice like a bull, and I wondered that he had not used it, as he was in the habit of doing in all cases of peril or emergency. The worst fear I had was, that he had fallen overboard; for it seemed to me that nothing else could have prevented him from halloing. But I had strong hopes that the next bend of the stream would remove my anxiety.

With the board I had torn from my raft I paddled with all my might; but it seemed like an hour to me, in my deep solicitude for the fate of my companions, before I reached the bend. At this point the stream made a sharp turn, and I had the intense satisfaction of seeing the light on the raft, on the right bank of the stream. The current set my craft directly towards it, and I had only to use my paddle in keeping it from whirling round.

A heavy load of anxiety was removed from my mind; but, as I approached the light, I wondered that Sim was not on the lookout for me. I ran alongside, and leaped upon the platform; but my clumsy assistant did not present himself to give me a welcome. A cold chill crept through my veins again, as I thought that he might have tumbled into the water, and been swept away by the current. The door of the house was closed, as I had left it, in order to keep the night air from Flora. Dreading lest some mishap had overtaken her also, I pushed the door open and rushed in.

My fears had been vain and foolish. Flora sat in her arm-chair at the stove, just as I had so often seen her in the kitchen of Captain Fishley, as calm and composed as though she had been on the dry land. Opposite her Sim Gwynn sat on the floor, fat and happy, and wholly undisturbed.

"What are you about, Sim?" I demanded, sharply; for I was vexed to see him taking it so coolly, while I had almost worried the life out of me.

"About nothin'; been waiting for you," replied my deck hand, with his customary grin.

"What did you let the raft go adrift for?"

"I didn't let it go adrift."

"Why didn't you keep her up to the shore?"

"She kept herself there."

"No, she didn't."

"Well, she's here—isn't she?"

"She is here, just where she ought not to be," I added, puzzled by the apparent stupidity of Sim. "You ought to stay outside when I leave you to take care of her."

"Miss Flora called me in to have me tell her what the matter was, and she kept talking to me ever since," pleaded Sim.

"Don't scold him, Buckland. It was my fault; but I did not know anything was wrong," interposed Flora.

"I'm not scolding him; but he should look out for the raft when I leave her in his care."

"Well, I did look out for it. It didn't run away from me, and here it is."

"If it didn't run away from you, it ran away with you."

"No, it didn't; here it is just as you left it."

"But the raft has come down stream more than half a mile since I left it."

"Hookie! What's that?" asked Sim, opening his eyes.

"Didn't you know the raft had broken loose, and travelled down stream half a mile or more?" I asked, filled with astonishment.

"I didn't know anything at all about it," protested Sim, vigorously.

"I'm sure I did not know that she had moved an inch," added Flora.

"That's strange," I continued, laughing. "When I came out of the swamp, I couldn't find the raft, and I was afraid you would get to New Orleans before I could catch you. Then I feared Sim had fallen overboard; and I suffered a great deal in a very short time."

"I heven't been out of the house since you went away, and I heven't the leastest idee that we were goin' on," said Sim. "I'll stay outside next time."

"You must, Sim; for we shall never know where we are if you don't keep your eyes wide open."

"What was it about the money, Buckland? Sim said you had forgotten your money; but he did not know what you meant by it," asked Flora.

I explained what I meant, and that I had concealed my money in the swamp to prevent the constable or the captain from finding it upon me.

"I am so sorry I called Sim!" pleaded poor Flora.

"It's no matter now. Perhaps it will be a good lesson for him and me to learn at the start. Now we will push off and try again. It is lucky I thought of the money when I did, for we could do nothing without that. Come, Sim, bear a hand!"

"Buckland, can't I step out and see the raft go?" asked Flora. "I don't like to stay in here."

"I'm afraid you will catch cold."

"No; I will wrap myself up in a blanket. I want to see how you manage the raft."

I could not refuse her; and, wrapping her up in a blanket, I carried her chair out to the side of the raised platform, and seated her in it. Sim and I took the boards from the small raft, which had been so useful to us in the swamp, and let the logs go adrift.

"Now take your pole, Sim, and push her off."

"She won't come off," replied the deck hand, after he had used all his power in the attempt to shove her off.

I went forward, and found the end of the raft had run upon the root of a tree, which held it fast. I was very grateful for the service this root had rendered me, for the raft might have gone down to Riverport before Sim discovered that anything was the matter. Fixing the poles underneath, we pried the raft off, and the current started it on its course again. I mounted the steering platform, and grasped the long oar. The voyage had actually commenced.

My position was a novel one, for I had yet to learn even the art of managing a raft. I found she had the same tendency to whirl around in the current which had characterized her smaller counterpart; but the oar was long enough to give the steersman a tremendous purchase, and the erratic disposition of the craft could be overcome when taken in season. I had to profit by experience, for before we reached the creek she had whirled round three times, in spite of all my efforts to prevent it. Before the raft was half way to Riverport, I had acquired the needed skill, and she indulged in no more gyrations while I had the helm.

As we approached the steeples of Riverport, I heard the clock strike one. Flora still sat in her chair by the platform, wondering how I could see to steer the raft, and asked me a thousand questions. I tried to have her go to bed, but she was not willing to do so till we had reached the Wisconsin River, which she desired to see.

We were all excited, and did not feel sleepy. Sim took a luncheon, and declared he never felt better in his life. It was the best fun he had ever known, and he enjoyed every moment of it. Flora said she liked it very much, but thought it would be pleasanter in the daytime, when the ever-changing scene could be viewed in the sunshine.

"I'm sure I shall be happy on the raft for a month," she added. "There will be something new to be seen every day."

"And we shall pass ever so many towns and cities, and the river will be full of steamers and flat-boats," I continued, as the raft glided round the bend into the great river. "Now we are in the Wisconsin, Flora; and this is Riverport on the right of us."

"We can't see much of it."

"No; but you will find enough in the daytime to amuse you. I hope you will sleep all night after this."

"I will go to bed now, Buckland," said she. "Good night."

"Good night, Flora."

She went into the house, and I heard nothing more from her till morning. I know that she prayed for me that night, as she always did; and I looked up to the shining stars, and commended her to the good Father. More than ever before did I love her then, when her life and happiness were more directly the care and study of my existence.

We were now on the broad river—broad compared with the creek, but small in contrast with the mighty Mississippi, which we were yet to see. Sim was forward, watching the dark outlines of the shores. Everything was quiet without, though my bosom still bounded with excitement. I could not forget that I was navigating the clumsy craft in which I had embarked my fortunes, and which held the being most dear to me on earth. I felt that a heavy responsibility rested upon me. Not a sound was to be heard except the gentle ripple of the waters against the sides of the raft; and the season was favorable to reflection.

But if the season was, Sim was not. He began to be weary of the solemn silence and the deep gloom of the hour, and came aft to talk with me. I saw that it would be necessary to keep him busy, in order to save him from his own reflections, and the dulness which was sure to follow. There was work enough on the raft to keep us both employed, and he was in no danger of dying from inaction.

"Are you going to keep her a-going all night, Buck?" asked he, in a tone so loud that it seemed to reverberate over the broad prairies which bounded the river.

"Hush, Sim! Don't talk so loud," I replied, in a whisper. "You will keep Flora awake if you do."

"Hookie! I didn't think of her," said he, slapping his great fist over his mouth, in token of his intention to do better.

"We shall keep moving, night and day, Sim."

"Are you always going to set up all night?" he whispered.

"No; you must do it half the time. You must learn to steer, and you may as well begin now."

"But I don't know how."

"You must learn."

"I don't think I can. I ain't much at anything except hard work."

"Take the oar, Sim, and try your hand at it. I had to learn, and you must do the same."

He took hold of the oar with me, while I, in a low tone, explained to him how to manage it. I then left it to his care. As I expected, he permitted the raft to whirl around.

"I told you I couldn't do it," said he, in disgust.

"Keep trying. When you see her head going one way, put the oar in the same direction. Don't wait till she is half round, but take her when she first begins to wabble," I added, assisting him to get the raft into position again.

But Sim did better than I had anticipated, and in half an hour he declared that he had "got the knack of the thing." I watched him for a while, until I had entire confidence in his ability. He was not so wide awake as he had been earlier in the night, and some fearful gapes suggested what he needed most. I had fixed up a bed for him on the floor of the house, and I found that he was quite willing to turn in when I gave him permission to do so. His excitement had died out suddenly; but I had no doubt of his zeal when the time for the hard work should come.

I was not sleepy, or even tired, myself; and hour after hour, till the daylight came, I stood at my post, solitary and alone, busy with thoughts of the present and the future. The steering of the raft was merely mechanical, after I became accustomed to it. I was glad to see the morning light, and to hear the song of the spring birds. The sun rose bright and beautiful, but my fellow-voyagers still slept. I enjoyed the scene, and I permitted them to slumber as long as they would.

CHAPTER XVIII.

AT THE MOUTH OF THE OHIO.

IT must have been eight o'clock when Flora opened the window of her room. She told me she had slept soundly, and felt as well as ever she did in her life. I think Sim would have snored till noon if I had not called him; but he had slept at least six hours, and I concluded that he could stand it till night. I gave him the steering oar, and Flora and I got breakfast. Our first meal on board was not entirely satisfactory, for we had no table, and only one chair.

I took the helm again while Sim ate his breakfast, and then went to bed myself; for I found, after my night of watching and excitement, I was in no condition to work. My companions were as considerate of me as I had been of them, and permitted me to sleep till the middle of the afternoon. I was "as good as new" then; and, after we had dined, I put up a table, and made a couple of stools.

During the day, we met two steamboats, and passed a huge flat-boat loaded with grain; but no one on board of them seemed to take any particular notice of us. Every kind of a craft is seen on the great western rivers, and none is so strange as to excite a sensation in the mind of the beholder. At six o'clock we had been afloat about twenty hours; and, according to my estimate, it was nearly time for us to see the Mississippi. The Wisconsin had widened as we advanced, and I was sure that we should be in the great river before midnight.

After supper, I discussed with Sim the subject of keeping watch during the night, and we decided that four hours were enough for each of us to steer at one time. But we had no means of measuring time in the night, and we could only guess at the length of the watch. I was to serve from eight till twelve, and Sim from twelve till four, when I was to take my place again.

Flora retired early on the second night, and I sent Sim to bed as soon as it was fairly dark. I was alone again, in the solitude of that waste of waters. The novelty of the scene had in some measure worn off. I had nothing but my own thoughts to amuse me. The river appeared still to be widening, and, as I had anticipated, before my watch had ended, the raft entered the Mississippi. The river was high, the current much stronger than it had been in the Wisconsin, and the progress of the raft was correspondingly increased. I met a steamboat struggling against the stream, and passed quite near to her. The swell that she left behind her caused the raft to roll heavily for a moment; but it did not disturb the sleepers in the house.

I called Sim at twelve o'clock, as nearly as I could judge, and he faithfully promised me that he would keep awake till daylight. I left him alone on the platform, and turned in, though not without some doubts in regard to his ability to be true to his promise. I went to sleep very promptly, and I must do Sim the justice to say that I found the raft all right when he called me at sunrise, an hour later than the time agreed upon. He told me that nothing had happened during the night, except that a steamboat had nearly upset the raft.

I do not intend to make a daily record of our voyage down the river. One day was very much like the next day, and all days were alike. On the afternoon of the first day on the Mississippi, we approached a village, where there was a steamboat landing. We were in want of supplies for our table, and I decided to stop for an hour or two. But I found that it was an easier matter to go ahead than it was to stop, for the raft had got into the habit of doing so. The water was too deep to permit the use of poles, and we were helplessly carried past the village.

I was vexed at this mishap, for I did not like to drink my coffee without milk. However, we came to another and a larger village about sundown, and, making my calculations in good season, I succeeded in driving the raft into the shallow water where we could use the poles. We struck the shore some distance above the place; but a walk of half a mile was not objectionable, after our long confinement on the raft.

At this town I purchased a cheap clock, and an old, patched sail, which had been used on a wood-boat, as well as some provisions and groceries. Sim and I lugged these articles to the raft, and immediately cast off again. I put the clock up in the house, where it could be seen through the door without leaving the platform. The lantern hung over it, so that we could tell the time by night.

I had great hopes of the sail, and the next day I rigged it upon two poles, serving as yards. On one corner of the sail I found a block, which had been used for the sheet. I fastened it at the masthead, so that we could hoist and lower the sail at pleasure. I was no navigator, and no sailor; and I had to experiment with the sail and rigging for a long while before I could make them work to my satisfaction.

My inventive powers did not fail me, and by attaching a rope to each end of the two yards, I obtained the control of the canvas. When I had completed the work, and hoisted the sail, I was delighted with its operation. The wind came pretty fresh from the north-west, and I think the raft made five, if not six miles an hour with its help. With the sail drawing well, the labor of steering was reduced more than half. The raft had no tendency to whirl round, and it was really a pleasure to steer her. We were not obliged to follow the current in its broad sweeps around the bends of the river, and we saved many miles by taking "short cuts." I found, too, that the raft was under better control, and, instead of being at the mercy of the current, we could go where we pleased. When there was any wind, and it came from the right direction, I could make a landing where and when I wished with very little difficulty.

Day after day we continued on our voyage, Sim and I dividing equally between us the labor at the steering oar. We could not use the sail all the time, but it was a vast help to us when the wind was favorable. As time permitted, I made improvements on the house, which added to our comfort. I put up two berths, which we filled with hay obtained from the prairies. I made a closet for the dishes, and a well in the body of the raft, where the kettle of milk could be kept cool in the water.

We made a landing almost every day at some town, and on Sunday we hauled up and went to church, whenever we were in a place where we could do so. On our sixth day it rained in torrents, and I hauled up at the bank of a river, and made fast to a tree. It was not comfortable to stand on the platform, wet to the skin, and steer. Sim and I slept nearly the whole day, while Flora read the books and newspapers which I had bought at the towns. I had done all the work I could find to do on the raft, and had fitted up the house to my mind. I had an easy time of it.

At one of the large towns I found what was called "A Panorama of the Mississippi River," which I bought and put up in the house. After this we knew just where we were, for the Panorama was a kind of chart, with all the towns on the river, the streams which flowed into it, and the distances from place to place, indicated upon it. With a good breeze we made about a hundred miles in twenty-four hours, and when we could not use the sail, the current carried us sixty miles.

When we reached the mouth of the Missouri, the prospect seemed to me, who had never seen a considerable body of water, to be like a great inland sea. Flora was appalled at our distance from the land, and Sim shouted, "Hookie!" Our raft, which had seemed so large on the stream where it had been built, now loomed puny and insignificant. Great steamboats, three times as large as any I had ever seen, and looming up far above the water, dashed by us. Huge flat-boats floated lazily down the river, and the scene became more lively and exciting as we advanced. A new world had opened to us.

From the broad river we saw the great city of St. Louis, and we gazed with wonder and astonishment at its dense mass of houses, its busy levee, and the crowds of steamboats which thronged it. We had never seen the great world before, and we were overwhelmed with surprise. Flora was silent, and Sim cried "Hookie" a hundred times within an hour.

The swift current and the steady breeze carried us away from this stormy scene into the quiet of nature; for the great river has its solitudes, though many times in the day we saw steamboats going up and down, or encountered other craft voyaging towards the Gulf.

On the tenth day we approached the mouth of the Ohio. Again the expanse of waters increased, till it seemed to my narrow vision to be almost an ocean. It was nearly dark, and the weather was as pleasant as a maiden's dream. We had advanced about seven degrees of latitude towards the south, and Nature was clothed in her brightest green. We had stepped from the cold spring of Wisconsin to the mild summer of the South. Ten days before we had been among leafless trees; now we were in the midst of luxuriant foliage. Flora sat in her arm-chair, near the platform, enjoying the scene with me.

"If you are tired of the raft, Flora, we will go the rest of the way in a steamboat," I said, after we had spoken of the changing seasons we had experienced.

"I am not tired of it—far from it," she replied.

"We have over a thousand miles farther to go."

"I think I shall only regret the river was not longer when we get to New Orleans."

"I wonder what Captain Fishley thinks has become of us," I added, chuckling, as I thought of the family we had left.

"He and his wife must be puzzled; but I suppose they won't find out where we are till we write to them."

"They will not know at present then. We have got rid of our tyrants now, and I am in no hurry to see them again."

"Twig the steamers!" shouted Sim, from the roof of the house, where he had perched himself to observe the prospect. "They are having a race."

I had seen them before, and I wished they had been farther off, for one of them seemed to be determined to run over the raft, in her efforts to cut off her rival. Our craft was in the middle of the channel, and one of the steamers passed on each side of us, and so close that we were nearly swamped in the surges produced by their wheels. I breathed easier when the boats had passed, for I knew how reckless they were under the excitement of a race. I could hear them creak and groan under the pressure, as they went by.

We watched them as they rushed forward on their course. They were just rounding into the Ohio, on their mad career, when we saw one of them suddenly fly in pieces, torn, rent, shivered, the atmosphere filled with fragments. Then came a terrific explosion, like the din of an earthquake, shaking the raft with its violence. The boiler of the steamer had exploded.

CHAPTER XIX.

AFTER THE EXPLOSION.

WHEN the explosion occurred, the wind was nearly dead ahead, and we were floating with the current, which was the particular reason why we had come so near being run down by the contestants.

"What's the matter?" asked Flora, alarmed by the noise, but unable to explain the cause of it.

"One of those steamers has burst her boiler. Didn't you see the pieces fly?" I replied.

"But where are the people we saw laughing and talking as she went by?" continued she, with a shudder.

"A good many of them will never laugh and talk any more."

"Hookie!" shouted Sim, as soon as he comprehended the nature of the disaster. "That's wus'n fallin' in the river."

"Get out the sail, Sim!" I added, sharply.

"What you want the sail for?" inquired he. "The wind ain't right for it."

"Up with it, and we will talk about that afterwards."

Letting go the steering oar, I hastened to Sim's assistance, while the raft whirled in the current as she went down the mighty river. We hoisted the sail, hauled in the braces, and I took my place on the platform again. After no little labor at the steering oar, I succeeded in putting the raft before the wind, thus heading her up the river.

"What are you going to do, Buckland?" asked Flora, who was watching the scene of the accident with the most painful interest.

"Hundreds of those poor people have already perished, and more will be drowned, unless they have some help," I replied, much excited. "I am going to try and get up there, so as to be of some service."

"O, I hope you will! But there are boats out picking them up already," added she, wringing her hands, as she realized more vividly the nature of the terrible catastrophe.

"I'm going to do all I can," I replied, thrilled by the exciting scene, which, though a mile distant, we could understand and realize.

I expected the hull of the steamer would float down the river with the swift current, bringing with it all its fearful surroundings; but in her haste to outstrip her competitor, she had run into the shallow water, and when riven by the explosion, had sunk. The awful scene, therefore, did not come down the stream, as I anticipated. In a few moments, three steamboats, besides the one which had been engaged in the race, were hovering about the wreck, and at least a dozen boats were busy in picking up the sufferers.

I found that it was utterly impossible to make any progress against the current with the raft. Though the wind was tolerably fresh from the southward, and the sail drew well, it barely held its own. The wreck and the raft remained about the same distance apart as at the moment of the explosion. But it was a consolation to know that our services were not absolutely needed, so abundant was the assistance afforded from the shore, and from the passing steamers.

In a short time parts of the wreck began to come down the river. We picked up a broken door, and other pieces of the wood-work, but nothing of any great value. We kept a sharp lookout for any survivors who might have been overlooked by the boats about us; but as yet we saw none, or even any who had been killed. Finding we could be of no service, I was about to turn the raft, and resume our voyage, when Flora called my attention to an object floating at some distance from us.

"It's a woman, Buckland!" exclaimed she, clasping my arm with convulsive energy.

"So it is," I replied, with my heart almost in my throat.

We were all too young and inexperienced to behold a human being apparently at the gates of death without a tremendous sensation of horror.

"Hookie!" gasped Sim, after he had gazed an instant at the object, his breath collapsing as he uttered the favorite expression.

"Can't you save her?" cried Flora, in trembling tones.

"I will if I can."

"O, do save her. It's terrible."

"She is clinging to a piece of wood, and has her head quite out of water," I added, as I turned the raft.

The unfortunate person was still some distance farther up the stream than the raft. I told Sim to trim the sail, and I hoped to get my clumsy craft in such a position that the current would bring the woman towards it, so that we could intercept her.

"Help! Help!" called the sufferer, in faint and fearful tones, as we came nearer to her.

"Hold on a few moments longer," I replied.

"I can't!" she answered, evidently chilled by the cold, and exhausted by her fruitless struggles.

"Only a moment," I added.

That moment was a fearfully long one, and at the end of it came failure. The raft disappointed me. The current was bearing the helpless female by it, but not more than fifty feet distant. It might as well have been a mile, so far as our capacity to overcome the space between us was concerned.

"Down with the sail, Sim!" I shouted, sharply.

"Hookie!" gasped Sim, still standing with his mouth wide open, gazing at the poor woman.

"Down with it!" I repeated, giving him a kick to sharpen his wits.

He stumbled to the sail; but his fingers were all thumbs, and he could not untie the halyard. I was obliged to do it myself, for the sail had filled aback, and it was retarding the progress of the raft.

"Help! Save me!" cried the unhappy person again, but fainter than before, as hope appeared to desert her.

"Hold on a moment more!" I shouted to her.

I grasped the steering oar, and vainly struggled to turn the raft, so as to bring it near enough to the sufferer to enable me to haul her on board; but the only effect was to cause it to whirl in the current. Both the woman and our craft were carried along by the stream, fifty feet apart; but neither had the power to approach any nearer to the other.

"I'm sinking!" called the woman, throwing one of her hands up into the air.

"No! Hold on for your life!" I shouted, as loud as I could scream.

My voice had some effect upon her, for she grasped the stick to which she was clinging.

"O, Buckland!" cried Flora, wringing her hands and sobbing hysterically. "Can't you do something?"

"I can, and will!" I replied, with some of the earnestness that thrilled my soul; and I felt that I ought to die myself rather than permit the poor sufferer to perish before my eyes.

"Do!" gasped my poor sister; and I knew she would have sacrificed her precious life to save that of the stranger.

"Come here, Sim!" I called.

My blundering deck hand came promptly at my call, and I gave him the steering oar, bidding him keep the raft steady before the current. I took the long lines, which I used as mooring ropes, and tied them together, making a cord at least a hundred feet in length. I took off all my clothes but my pants and shirt, and secured the cord around my body, making fast the other end to the raft.

"Sim!" said I, startling him with the sharpness of my tones.

"Yes; I'm here, Buck! Hookie!" stammered he.

"Mind what you're about!"

"O, yes! I will!"

"When I tell you, let go the oar, and pull in on this rope."

"I'll help him," said Flora.

"Don't you touch the rope, Flora. You may get dragged overboard."

"What shall I do?"

"You may make a fire in the stove, if you can," I answered, wishing to get her out of the reach of danger if I could.

"I will, Buckland;" and she went into the house.

I was a powerful swimmer, and nerved by the peril of the stranger in the water, I felt able to do anything. I let myself down into the river, and struck out with all my strength towards the sufferer. The current of the Mississippi is swift and treacherous. It was the hardest swimming I had ever known; and, dragging the rope after me, I had a fierce struggle to make any progress. In going those fifty feet, it seemed to me that I worked hard enough to accomplish a mile.

I reached the sufferer, and grasped the stick to which she clung. I was nearly exhausted myself by the violence of my efforts. I waited a moment to regain my breath, before I attempted to deal with the difficulties of the situation. I glanced at the person for whom I was to struggle. She was not a woman, but a girl of fourteen. She was in a sinking condition, apparently more from the effects of fear than actual suffering, for the stick to which she clung afforded her ample support.

Afraid that the act of hauling us in would detach her from the stick, I grasped it firmly with one hand, and clasped her around the waist with the other. Her frame quivered with the cold and the terror of her situation. As all persons in peril of drowning are apt to do, she was disposed to cling to me.

"Don't be afraid," said I to her. "You are safe now."

"Save me!" gasped she, hardly loud enough to be heard.

"Haul in!" I shouted to Sim.

I felt the rope cutting my waist as Sim jerked and tugged at it with all his strength. There was no lack of zeal on his part, but if anything had depended upon coolness and skill, we might both have been drowned. I kept a firm hold upon my helpless charge, and managed to keep her head above the water, though my own was dragged under several times by the clumsiness of my willing friend.

Sim pulled and hauled with energy, if not with skill. When he abandoned the steering oar, the raft began to whirl, and thus to complicate his labor. I caught a glance of the simple-minded fellow, as the craft turned, and I heard him yell, "Hookie!" He was nonplussed by the change of the raft; but he did not know enough to follow it round upon the outside. I am not sure this freak of the current did not save us from a calamity, for as it revolved, and the rope became tangled in the platform, we were thrown against the raft, thus saving my helpmate half his toil. Fortunately the end of the stick on which I floated struck the logs first, and broke the force of what might otherwise have been a stunning blow.

"Tie the rope, Sim!" I called to my assistant, who was now on the other side of the raft.

"O, Buckland!" cried Flora, as she came out of the house and gazed at me with an expression of intense pain.

"Hookie!" ejaculated Sim, rushing to the point where I had seized hold of the raft.

AFTER THE EXPLOSION.

He stood there, jumping up and down on both feet, bewildered and helpless.

CHAPTER XX.

EMILY GOODRIDGE.

IN the water, struggling for his own or another's life, a man's stock in trade consists mainly of breath. Without that he can't do much, and generally he fails for the want of it; not when life deserts him, but when he might, by an economical use of it, have been able to save himself. I had been in the water enough to learn this lesson, and to be competent to advise all my young friends, in the moment of peril, to refrain from useless and unreasonable struggling, for that wastes the breath, and fritters away the strength.

I held on at the raft till I had recovered my breath, and felt strong enough to make another effort; for I found that my own life and that of my charge were to depend principally on my own exertions. Sim was willing, but he was stupid; and I was afraid that some blunder of his would yet lose me the battle.

I brought the helpless girl on my arm so that she could take hold of the raft, but she seemed not to have the power to do so.

"Sim, mind what you are about now!" I called to my help.

"I will, Buck! What shall I do?" stuttered he.

"Lie down on the platform so that you can reach the girl."

He obeyed, and held out his great paws towards my helpless burden. I raised her up a little, and he grasped her under the arms. He was as strong as an ox; and raising her a little way, he turned over, and then lifted her clear from the water, but dragging her up as roughly as though she had been a log of wood. I needed no help myself, and was on the raft almost as soon as the girl. She was utterly exhausted, and unable to hold up her head. Sim and I carried her into the house. We laid her in Sim's bunk, and Flora was as tender with her as though she had been a baby.

"Hookie!" exclaimed Sim, staring at the sufferer, with his mouth open wide enough to take in a canal boat. "Is she dead?"

"No—not dead!" replied Flora, as she lifted the wet locks from her face, and gently rubbed her temples. "What shall we do for her, Buckland?"

"She is chilled with the cold, and worn out with fear and exertion."

"I shall be better soon," said the girl, faintly. "I feel better now. Let me rest a moment."

"Give her some hot tea," suggested Flora.

The tea-pot was on the stove, and I prepared a cup of tea for her. She drank it, and the effect was good.

"I feel better; but I am so cold!" said she.

Flora and I consulted what it was best to do, and we finally decided that her wet clothing must be removed. I carried her into my sister's room, and laid her on a blanket. I then closed up the shutters of the outer room, replenished the fire, and left Flora to do the rest. The stove would heat the house as hot as an oven when the windows and doors were closed.

Sim was now at the steering oar, where I joined him. Except the fragments of the wreck which floated on the river, there was no vestige of the terrible calamity in sight.

"Do you think she will die?" asked Sim, looking as anxious as though the girl had been one of our own party.

"No; she is better now. She will be all right in a day or two."

"Who is she?" asked he, opening his mouth and his eyes to express his wonder.

"I don't know—how should I?"

"Didn't she tell you?"

"No—she isn't able to talk much yet. She hasn't said ten words."

"Didn't she tell you who she was?"

Sim asked silly questions, and I had not always the patience to answer him, especially when he had asked the same ones half a dozen times. I had as much curiosity as he had to know who and what the young lady was, and I was impatient to hear from Flora. As she did not call me, I was satisfied her patient was doing well. It was quite dark now, and I was walking rapidly up and down the raft, to keep myself warm, for I had had no opportunity to change my wet clothes for dry ones.

"Buckland!" called the soft voice of Flora, "You may come in now."

"How is the girl?" I asked.

"She is nicely now. I have rubbed her, put dry clothes upon her, and covered her up with blankets in my bed. She wants to see you."

I followed Flora into her room. The stranger, with the exception of her head, was buried in the blankets, and by the dim light of the lantern I saw as pretty a face as it ever had been my good fortune to behold before. I had hardly seen her until now; certainly my first impressions of her features and expression were derived from this observation, rather than from any former one. She had a very mild, soft blue eye; but she looked quite sad and troubled.

"I wish to tell you how grateful I am to you for saving my life," said she. "I shall never forget your kindness, and I hope I may be able to do something more for you."

"O, never mind that," I replied. "That's all right. I'm glad I had a chance to do as I did."

"You are a brave and noble young man, and you saved my life. It may do for you to forget it, but it will not do for me to do so."

"I won't complain if you do;" and as all heroes say under similar circumstances, I told her I had only done my duty.

"Yet I almost wish you had not saved me," she added, with a shudder, as her eyes suddenly filled with tears.

"Why so?" I asked, though I had not much difficulty in reading the cause of her sadness.

"My mother! O, my mother!" cried she, in agony.

Poor girl! I wanted to cry with her. Flora threw her arms around her neck, and wept with her.

"Your mother was in the steamer—was she?" I added.

"She was—and lost."

"Perhaps not," I suggested.

"O, I know she was."

"Probably some were saved."

"I dare not hope so," sobbed she, uncovering her eyes, and glancing at me. "I was sitting clear back, as far as I could get, looking into the water, when this terrible thing happened. I was thrown into the river by the shock, or I jumped in—I don't know which. I caught hold of that stick, but I did not know what I was doing."

"But where was your mother?" I asked. "She may have been equally fortunate."

"The boat was racing with another, and Mr. Spear asked my mother to go forward, and see the furnaces under the boilers, which, he said, were red hot. I was reading a book, and did not want to go. In two or three minutes after they went, the boiler burst. My mother must have been very near the furnaces when the explosion took place."

"Who was Mr. Spear?"

"He was the gentleman who was taking charge of us."

"But it is possible that your mother was saved."

"I wish I knew!" she exclaimed, with tremulous emotion. "Can't you ascertain? I shall be so grateful to you!"

"I will try," I replied. "We are not more than ten miles from the place where the accident happened, and I can return."

"O, I wish you would!"

"Do you wish to return?" I asked.

"She cannot go to-night," interposed Flora. "She is all worn out."

"I do not feel able to go," added the poor girl; "and I do not wish to go unless my mother is saved."

"What is your mother's name?"

"Mrs. Goodridge."

"And yours?"

"Emily Goodridge."

"Where do you live?"

"In New Orleans. My father is a merchant there. I have been sick, and the doctor said I must go to the North; but my mother—"

She could say no more, for her sobs choked her utterance. I assured her I would do all I could to ascertain the fate of her mother. I went into the other room, and changed my clothes, and wrote down the names which Emily gave me, so that I need not forget them. After assuring myself that everything was right in the house, I went out and hoisted the sail. Taking the steering oar, I ran the raft up to the shore on the Missouri side, as the wind was favorable in that direction. I secured the craft in the strongest manner, in order to make sure that she did not go adrift during the night.

I knew there was a village not far above, for I had seen the lights of it through the window as I was talking to Emily. I went on shore, and walked about a mile, which brought me to the place. I went into a store that I found open on the levee, and inquired of the keeper in what manner I could get to Cairo. He told me I could only go by a steamboat, and that I might have to wait an hour, or a couple of days, for one. But, while I was talking with him, a man came in and said there was a boat coming up the river. The person who brought this pleasing intelligence was rough looking, and I offered him a dollar if he would put me on board of her. He accepted my proposition so good-naturedly that I concluded the boat was coming up to the town; but she did not, and he put me into a bateau, and pulled off to her. At first she would not stop.

"Great news!" I shouted, at the top of my lungs.

Curiosity did what good-nature would not, and the boat stopped her wheels long enough for me to jump on her deck.

"What do you mean by great news?" demanded a gentleman, who, I soon found, was the captain. "Did you say that to make me stop the boat? If you did, I'll heave you overboard."

"No, sir; I did not," I replied, with becoming promptness after the threat he had used.

"What's your great news, then?" demanded he.

"Do you know what two steamers went up the river about two or three hours ago?" I asked.

"Certainly I do—the River Queen No. 4 and the Centurion. They passed me this morning. But what's your news, boy?"

"The Centurion blew up about seven o'clock, as she was going into the Ohio River."

"The Centurion!" exclaimed he.

"Yes, sir."

"Is that so, or are you making up this story?"

"It is true, sir. I saved a young lady who was a passenger. I left her below this village, and I want to go up and find out whether her mother was lost, or not."

"What is her name?"

"Emily Goodridge."

"Goodridge? Do you know her father's name?"

I looked at my paper, and found the name was Edward F. Goodridge.

"He is one of the heaviest merchants in New Orleans," added the captain, thoughtfully.

My news proved to be all I had represented it, and I was plied with questions which I could not answer, by the passengers interested in the fate of those on board of the unfortunate steamer. I could only tell them that the boat had been blown all to pieces, and that there was plenty of assistance at hand to save those who were thrown into the water.

In less than an hour my news was fully confirmed on the arrival of the steamer at Cairo. We were informed that the River Queen No. 4 was still there, with the survivors of the disaster on board, and I hastened to find her.

CHAPTER XXI.

FLORA AND HER PATIENT.

THERE was no difficulty, in finding the River Queen No. 4, for she was the centre of a circle of melancholy interest, and a crowd of people had gathered on the levee to hear the latest tidings of woe from her cabin, now changed into a hospital. I care not to dwell upon the sad scene which greeted my vision as I went on board of her, nor to describe the horror with which I glanced at the long row of ghastly corpses which had been taken from the water.

It was a sickening sight, and terrible were the groans and the wailings of the sufferers which resounded through the boat. I learned that the captain of the ill-fated steamer was among the dead. If it had not been so, an hour in the midst of this horrible din of sighs, and wails, and groans would have been an all-sufficient punishment, if he had a human heart in his bosom, for the base crime of sacrificing those precious lives to the stupid rivalry of the hour.

The officers and passengers had been engaged in making up lists of the wounded and the dead. Among the latter I found the name of Mrs. Goodridge and Mr. Spear. I shuddered as I realized that the worst fears of Emily were confirmed. I informed the clerk of the boat that I had saved one of the passengers, and her name was stricken from the list of the dead, and added to that of the living.

I learned that the body of Mrs. Goodridge had been recovered, and that friends on board of the steamer would take charge of it. There was nothing more for me to do, and I fled, sick at heart, from the awful spectacle. I went to a small hotel near the landing, and though I slept heavily, awake or in my slumber, the scenes of death and woe I had beheld still haunted my mind. I took an early breakfast, and then endeavored to find a boat bound down the river. There was none in Cairo that would start that day, and it might be several days before I could obtain a passage. I could not think of prolonging the agonizing suspense of our passenger on the raft, or of leaving the two females to the care of so heavy a thinker as Sim Gwynn. If a squall or a sudden rise of the river occurred, my assistant would be helpless; and if the raft broke loose, he would not have wit enough to bring it up to the shore again.

I walked up and down the levee, thinking what I should do. I could not charter a steamer, and there was no conveyance on the other side of the Mississippi. While I was thus fretting at the delay, I came to a yard where boats were kept for sale. Most of them were for the use of steamers, and were far beyond my means; but I found a second-hand skiff, which I purchased for ten dollars, including in the price a pair of good oars. It would be a handy thing to have on the raft, and if I had had it when I first saw poor Emily Goodridge in the water, I could have saved her without any difficulty.

In this light boat I embarked at nine o'clock. The raft was ten or twelve miles below Cairo; but the swift current would speed me on my way with little labor at the oars. I pulled steadily, and with just power enough to give me steerage-way; and when I reached the raft, I found I had made the passage in little more than two hours.

"Hookie!" ejaculated Sim, with a stupid stare, as I ran the skiff up to the raft.

"Catch the painter!" I called, throwing him the rope.

"I hain't seen no painter," he replied, staring around him, and letting the rope run off the raft, and the skiff go adrift.

I pulled up to the raft again, and succeeded in making my deck hand understand that he was to hold on to the rope attached to the boat.

"Where did you get that boat?"

"Catch hold, and haul it up," I replied; for I seldom found it practicable to answer Sim's questions.

"Did you find this boat?" he asked when he had pulled it up on the platform.

"No; how is the girl we saved?"

"Did you make this boat?"

"No; I bought it; gave ten dollars for it. How is the girl?"

"O, she's sick! Leastwise, she ain't very well, and didn't sleep much."

I did not suppose she had slept very well; for one with such a fearful anxiety on her mind must have suffered intensely during the long night. I hastened into the house, and found dear Flora making some tea for her patient. I surmised that the poor child had also spent a sleepless night, for she looked pale and ill herself, and I trembled for her welfare, devoted and self-sacrificing as she was in the presence of the heavy woe of her charge.

"How is Emily?" I asked.

"She is very sick, I fear," replied poor Flora, sadly, for she seemed to make her patient's sufferings her own. "She has hardly closed her eyes during the night."

"And you have not slept yourself, Flora."

"No, I have not. The poor girl has talked about her mother all night long. What news do you bring, Buckland?"

"I hardly dare to speak it," I replied, in a whisper.

"It can be no worse that her fears. She is already reconciled to the worst," added my sister, with a sympathetic tear.

"Flora," moaned Emily.

The devoted little nurse hastened to her patient. I had not the courage to follow her, and face the torrent of woe which my news must carry to her aching heart. Perhaps it was cowardly in me, but I could not help it. I stood at the door and listened.

"Your brother has come. I heard his voice," said Emily, in a tone convulsed with emotion.

"He has come, dear," replied Flora; and I heard her kiss the grief-stricken maiden.

"You have no good news to tell me. I know you haven't," wailed the sufferer. "I did not expect any. I knew she was—"

And then I heard her sob. She was calmer than I had anticipated, and I ventured to go into the room. My heart was in my throat as I gazed upon her pale face and hollow eyes. She wept bitterly, as I confirmed her worst fears; and Flora, with her arm twined around the poor girl's neck, wept with her, and frequently kissed her. As gently and tenderly as I could I told her the sad truth, and assured her that kind friends had taken charge of her mother's remains.

I left her with Flora then, for she was the best comforter. As I put on my working clothes in the adjoining room, I heard my sweet sister speaking to her the tenderest of pious consolations. She breathed the name of Jesus in her ear, and pointed her to the Rock of Ages for hope, for the joy which this world cannot give and cannot take away. Great rough fellow as I was, I wept with them; for never had my heart been so deeply touched before.

On the platform I found Sim, still employed in examining the skiff I had purchased, apparently filled with astonishment that a little thing like that had borne me safely down the river for ten miles. He wanted to ask more questions about it; but I told him to cast off the fasts, and in a few moments we were again borne on by the current of the Father of Waters. The day was bright and pleasant, and a fresh wind from the north-west was blowing. I hoisted the sail and trimmed it, and taking my place at the steering oar, I brooded over the bitter lot of my passenger. I pitied her, and loved her for her misfortunes.

As the raft continued on its way, I began to consider what should be done with her. She was quite sick, and the rough house on the raft was not a suitable place for her. But she had no friends nearer than New Orleans. I asked myself whether I ought not to abandon the raft, and take passage in a steamboat; but I had not money enough to pay the passages of the party, and I was obliged to answer the question in the negative. But I could pay Emily's fare, and place her in charge of the officers of some boat. I concluded to adopt this course at the first large town we reached, where a steamer would be likely to make a landing.

The poor girl was unable to sit up during the day; indeed, she was so ill that I began to be alarmed about her. After dinner, I insisted that Flora should lie down on my bed, and obtain the rest she so much needed, while I sat with the patient. My poor sister was all worn out, and she slept till dark. Thanks to the gentle ministrations of Flora, Emily was quite calm, but she could not sleep. She talked to me of her mother all the time, and I became almost a woman myself in my efforts to console her.

I told her that I proposed to send her to New Orleans by the first steamer I could find which was bound there. To my surprise, she strongly objected, declaring that Flora was an angel, and she would not leave her. She said she was very comfortable on the raft, and that she was much happier there than she should be in a steamboat; and she trembled when she uttered the word. I told her that her father would be very anxious about her, and she finally decided to write a letter to him, informing him that she was in the hands of good friends, on her way home.

Flora was much refreshed by the sleep she had obtained, and sat up till midnight with Emily. I made a bed for her on the floor by the side of her patient, and in the morning I found that both of them had rested well during the latter part of the night. Sim and I kept the raft going all night, as usual. The next day I mailed Emily's letter to her father. The physical condition of the poor sufferer did not yet begin to improve, and Flora was unremitting in her efforts to help her. I was very much surprised to find that the devoted nurse did not sink under her exertions. But the patient slept tolerably well at night, and I relieved my sister during part of the day.

On the third day after the disaster, we passed Memphis; and I again urged Emily to take a steamer for her destination. She consented; but I found that she did so in order to save us the trouble she gave. When I assured her that we had no desire to get rid of her, she insisted upon completing the voyage on the raft. She could not bear to part with Flora, who had been both nurse and comforter to her in her affliction.

I made a landing at Memphis, and procured everything I could think of that would add to the comfort of Emily. She was very grateful to me, as well as to Flora, and I am free to say that I found my greatest happiness in caring for her and my sister; and all the more because they were so devoted to each other.

Day after day went by; and our course continued past Vicksburg, Natchez, Grand Gulf, Baton Rouge, till, on the thirteenth day from Cairo, and on the twenty-third from Torrentville, we came in sight of the spires of New Orleans.

The sun was just setting as we came abreast of the dense piles of houses. When we reached a place favorable for landing, I ran the raft up to the levee, and made it fast to a post.

CHAPTER XXII.

THE END OF THE VOYAGE.

FOR the week preceding the arrival of the raft, Emily Goodridge had been improving in health, though she was still quite feeble. She sat up part of the day, and spent an hour or two in the forenoon in the open air. As we approached the city, the excitement of being so near home buoyed her up, and seemed to give her an unnatural strength.

For my own part, I was in a whirl of excitement. The end of the voyage was a tremendous event in itself; but, as I thought of the astonishment of my brother when he should see Flora and me, and of the meeting between Mr. Goodridge and his daughter, I could hardly contain myself. The sights along the river, too, were sufficiently wonderful to keep my eyes wide open, and my heart leaping. For the first time in my life I saw a ship—hundreds of them, whose forest of masts and spars was as strange to me as though I had been transported to the centre of the Celestial Empire.

It seemed to me an age since I had left Torrentville; since, with bounding bosom, I had guided the raft down the creek to the Wisconsin. The events which had preceded our departure appeared to have occurred years ago, and to be dwarfed into littleness by the lapse of time. Captain Fishley, his wife, and Ham seemed almost like myths, so far removed were they from me by distance and time. I had almost forgotten that I had been charged with a base crime, and that I had fled to escape unpleasant consequences.

There was the great city of New Orleans spread out before me; and there, somewhere in the midst of its vast mass of heaving life, was my brother, and Flora's brother. I knew not where to look for him. But my first duty was to the poor girl, sick in body and sick at heart, who had voyaged down the river with us; who had made us feel enough of Christ's spirit to know that "it is more blessed to give than to receive."

Emily was in the chamber with Flora when Sim and I fastened the raft to the post. My fellow-laborer had already indulged in unnumbered "Hookies," and his eyes were set wide open by the wonders that surrounded us. I left him to stare, and to be stared at by the idlers on shore, and went into the house.

"Our journey is ended!" I exclaimed.

"And I am close to my father's house," added Emily, with convulsive emotion.

As I looked into her pale face, I could not help fearing that she was close to her Father's house in a higher sense than she meant the words—close to that "house of many mansions, eternal in the heavens;" for she seemed to have, in her weakness, but little hold upon this life.

"Where does your father live, Emily?" I asked.

"In Claiborne Street," she replied. "If you could get a carriage, I would like to go there at once."

"Do you feel able to ride in the carriage?"

"O, yes—to go home."

I went ashore, and soon found a carriage. I need hardly say that Emily's clothing was in very bad condition, though Flora had done what she could to improve it. Fortunately, it was nearly dark, and her appearance did not excite much attention. I could not permit her to go alone, and she insisted that Flora should accompany her. I left Sim in charge of the raft, with the promise to return soon. The carriage conveyed us to the number in Claiborne Street indicated by Emily. It was an elegant mansion, and I was abashed by the splendors that were presented to my view as I entered.

The coming of Emily created a sensation among the servants; but her father was not at home, though he was momentarily expected. Flora and I were conducted to a magnificent parlor, whose splendors exceeded anything of which I had ever dreamed. Emily went up stairs, to clothe herself properly before her father came. The poor girl wept bitterly as she entered the house which she had left three weeks before with her mother. The torrent of grief was renewed as she gazed again upon the familiar scenes which had always been so closely associated with the dear one who was gone.

A mulatto servant-man came into the room where Flora and I were. He had just greeted his young mistress, and his eyes were still filled with tears.

"We have been expecting Miss Emily for several days," said he. "Her father has suffered everything on her account."

"I am sorry she was delayed, but she would not leave my sister," I replied.

"But how did she come? It was a very slow steamer," he added.

"It was not a steamer. Didn't she write to her father?"

"Yes; but she didn't say what she was coming in; only that she was with very good friends, and should be home in a week or ten days."

"She came on a raft."

"On a raft!" exclaimed the man. "Miss Emily?"

"It was her own choice. I tried to have her take a steamer; but she would not. But there was a house on the raft, and she had a good bed."

"Of course her father has felt very bad, and since the funeral he has fretted a great deal about her."

"Since what funeral?" I asked.

"Her mother's. Poor Mrs. Goodridge was brought down from Cairo, packed in ice, and the funeral was a week ago yesterday."

One of the many steamers which passed us on our way down the river had brought the remains of Emily's mother, and they had already been committed to their last resting-place.

The ringing of the door-bell called the servant from us. We heard the heavy step of a man, as he went up stairs; but we did not witness the first interview between Emily and her father. They had much to say, and we did not see them for half an hour. When they entered the parlor together, both of them were tolerably calm; but the traces of tears were still visible in their eyes.

"Young man," said Mr. Goodridge, taking me by the hand, after Emily had introduced Flora and me by name, "I am indebted to you for the life of my child."

He wept, and could not utter what he evidently intended to say. My cheek burned, for in my sympathy for the poor girl and her father I had quite forgotten my hard swim after the disaster. I stammered some reply, and did not even then know what I was saying.

"Under God, you saved her; and I shall bless you as long as I live for the noble deed. It was hard to lose her who is gone; it would have been doubly hard to lose both of them."

"O, I don't think anything of what I did," I replied. "My poor little sister here has done a good deal more than I have for her."

Mr. Goodridge took the hand of Flora, and thanked her as he had thanked me. I told him the story of our voyage down the river after Emily joined us, as briefly as I could, giving my poor sister the credit for all her careful and devoted nursing of the invalid.

"I must go now, sir," I added, when the narrative was finished.

"Indeed, you must not," said the grateful father, decidedly.

"I left Sim Gwynn on the raft. He is rather simple, and I am afraid something will happen to him."

"Can't he leave the raft?"

"Not yet; my sister's clothes and other things are in the house."

He called the servant and ordered a carriage, saying he would go with me himself to the raft, and employ a man to take charge of it. We drove to the levee, where Mr. Goodridge sent for one of the porters in his warehouse, who was ordered to sleep on board, and see that nothing was stolen. Sim was directed to get into the carriage with us, and we went back to the house of the merchant.

"Hookie!" almost screamed Sim, as we entered the elegant mansion.

"Shut up, Sim! Don't open your mouth again!" I whispered to him.

"Hookie!" replied he, in a suppressed tone.

"Well, Buckland," said our host, when we were seated in the parlor,—Sim with his mouth open almost as wide as his eyes,—"I should like to know something more about you. You have only told me what occurred after you saved Emily. How happened you to be floating down the river on a raft?"

I told my story, from the day my father died, keeping back nothing except the matter relating to Squire Fishley's infirmity.

"And your brother is here in New Orleans?" said he.

"Yes, sir. He has gone into business here."

"What is his name?"

"Clarence Bradford."

"Bradford! I thought your name was Buckland."

"John Buckland Bradford, sir."

"I know your brother very well. He is the junior partner in the firm of Bent, La Motte, & Co. Their house is doing a fine business, too. I don't think we can find your brother to-night, but we will in the morning."

"He will be very much astonished to see us here."

"No doubt of it; but your coming was a blessing to me. I have three sons, but Emily is my only daughter, and the youngest child. She is my pet. She is in delicate health, and I tremble at the thought of losing her. You cannot understand what a service you have rendered me."

He was silent for several minutes, and I saw the tears starting in his eyes again. He was thinking of her who was lost, or her who was saved—of both, more likely.

"Shall you return to Torrentville again?" he asked, after walking across the room two or three times, apparently to quiet his emotions.

"No, sir, I think not."

"Wherever you go, young man, I shall be your friend, with my money and my influence."

"Thank you, sir."

"I will consult with your brother, to-morrow, in regard to what I can do to serve you best; but my gratitude shall have a substantial expression."

"O, sir, I don't ask anything for what I have done," I protested.

"You do not ask it; but that does not absolve me from doing something. But, to change the subject, I do not quite like to have you accused of robbing the mail."

"I didn't do it, sir."

"The gentleman who gave you the money ought to come forward and explain. If you didn't open the letter, you should not suffer a day for it. I will see your brother about that, too. It must be made right."

"I should be very glad to have it made right; but I can't tell who the man was that gave me the money."

He insisted, in very complimentary terms, that one who had done what I had could not be guilty of a crime, and that I must be cleared even from the suspicion of evil.

Sim and I slept on beds of down that night. The next morning Mr. Goodridge undertook to find Clarence. About the middle of the forenoon, while our raft party were all gathered in the parlor with the housekeeper, he was shown into the room. Not a word had been said to him as to the nature of the business upon which he was called, and his eyes opened almost as wide as Sim's when he saw Flora and me.

CHAPTER XXIII.

CLARENCE BRADFORD.

"MY dear little Flora!" exclaimed Clarence, as he glanced from me to her, after he entered the room.

He sprang to her chair, and embraced and kissed her. I perceived that he was winking rapidly, as though an unmanly weakness was getting possession of him.

"Buck!" he added, extending his hand to me, "what does all this mean? I supposed you were both in Torrentville."

"We are not. We couldn't stand it any longer," I replied.

"Stand what?" he demanded, sternly.

"The way that Captain Fishley's folks treated us."

"You don't mean to say they abused you!"

"That's just what I mean to say. I thought I spoke plain enough in my letters for you to understand me."

"I had no idea that you were actually abused. Boys are always grumbling and complaining, and some of them think their lot is a great deal harder than it is. Flora didn't say anything in her letters; she didn't complain."

"She wouldn't have said anything if they had killed her," I replied. "I am not one of the grumbling sort, and I didn't say anything till they picked upon me so that I couldn't stand it. I was kept at home from school half the time to work; and then I was the old man's servant, the old woman's servant, and Ham's servant. I was kept on the jump by some of them all the time."

"But you were only to take care of the horse, and go for the mail every evening; and I thought you rather liked that," he added; and he wore a look of astonishment and indignation.

"I did like it; but I had to work in the garden, feed the pigs, make the fires, do chores about the house, run of errands, and work in the store. I was kept busy from morning till night."

"That wasn't the bargain I made with them."

"I wouldn't have made any row about the work, if they hadn't treated me so meanly. Ham used me like a dog, and ordered me around as though I had been his nigger servant. It was 'Buck, do this,' and 'Buck, do that, and be quick about it.' It was 'Buck, black my boots,' in surly tones."

"Black his boots!" exclaimed Clarence.

"Yes, black his boots; and I was fool enough to do it until I found I only got kicked for minding. Mrs. Fishley used to snarl at me from morning till night. I never did anything right, and was never in the place where I ought to be. But, Clarence, I should have staid there, I suppose, till the time you named, if they had not abused Flora."

"Flora!" said he, knitting his brow, as he glanced at her.

I told him that our female tyrant had actually shaken her several times, to say nothing of the constant scolding to which she was subjected. He was indignant, and assured me, if he had supposed the case was half as bad as I had represented, he should have hastened to Torrentville and removed us at once. He thought my complaints were simply boyish dissatisfaction, and the situation nothing more than simply unpleasant.

"But you haven't told the worst of the story," interposed Mr. Goodridge.

"I will tell that now, for it was the final cause of our leaving," I continued. "A certain gentleman, whose name I cannot mention, gave me one hundred dollars for something I did for him."

"Who was he?" asked Clarence.

"I can't tell you, or anybody, who he was. About this time Ham Fishley robbed a letter of forty dollars, and when the money was missed, he laid it to me."

"How do you know he did it?" demanded Clarence.

"I saw him do it. I saw him break the seal, take out the money, and burn the letter;" and I explained fully the circumstances. "Ham saw me counting my money, and his father wanted me to tell where I got it. I couldn't do that. They sent for a constable; but I took to the swamp. Now, I had either to tell where I got the money,—which I couldn't do,—or go to jail. Instead of doing either, I took Flora on the raft with me, and came down the river."

"This is a very strange story, Buck; and I don't much blame Captain Fishley for not believing it," said Clarence. "Somebody gave you a hundred dollars, and you would not tell who, even to save yourself from going to jail. I can't blame him."

"Nor I either, so far as that was concerned; but I do blame Ham, for he knew very well that I did not rob the mail."

"But why can't you tell who gave you the money?"

"Because I promised not to do so, and because my telling would do an injury to the person who gave it to me."

"I don't like the looks of this thing, Buck," added Clarence, shaking his head.

"I know it don't look very well," I replied, rather sheepishly, for I realized that my brother had his suspicions.

"Why should a man give you a hundred dollars?"

"Because I saved his life," I answered, desperately.

"If you did, he ought to be the first one to give you the credit for the noble deed."

"There's the hitch."

"So I think," said my brother, shaking his head.

"Clarence, I know Buckland is honest and true," interposed Flora. "He is the best brother that ever was, and you mustn't think hard of him."

"Perhaps you know more about it than I do, Flora; but it looks bad for him. Why a man should give him a hundred dollars for saving his life, and then not be willing that he should mention his name, passes my comprehension."

"The gentleman had been drinking a little too much, and that was what made him fall into the water," I added, goaded on to reveal thus much by the doubts and suspicions of my brother.

"Well, that makes it a little more plausible," replied Clarence. "Was there no one present when the man fell overboard?"

"I shall not say any more about it, whether you believe it or not," I answered, rather indignantly. "I made a promise, and I intend to keep it."

"I am satisfied the young man is honest, Mr. Bradford," said the merchant.

"I know he is," added Emily, with an enthusiasm which was worth the testimony of all the others.

"After the noble deed he has done, after risking his life to save that of an entire stranger, as he did for my daughter, I know he is not capable of robbing the mail," continued Mr. Goodridge.

"Saved your daughter?" asked Clarence, with an inquiring look at Emily and her father.

Flora volunteered to tell the story of the events following the steamboat explosion, and my modesty will not permit me to set down the pleasant speeches which Emily added to the narrative.

"Well, Buck, I am willing to grant that you are a hero," said Clarence, good-naturedly; "and you have done things for which I should have been slow to give you the credit, if the facts were not fully attested by all these witnesses. So you have made a voyage from Torrentville to New Orleans on a raft?"

"I have, and brought Flora with me."

"You have proved yourself to be a smart boy, and I only wish you had left a better reputation behind you at Torrentville."

I thought this remark was a little harsh. I do not wish to say anything against my brother, but I was very much disappointed in the view which he took of the robbery question. I know that he valued reputation as the apple of his eye, and keenly felt that it was cowardice for an innocent person to run away from the appearance of evil. I know that he was very indignant at the treatment which the Fishleys had bestowed upon Flora and me; but he seemed to believe that I had exaggerated it, and that I had fled from Torrentville solely to escape the consequences of robbing the mail.

He was not satisfied with my conduct, and declared that my character must be cleared from all suspicion. The name he bore must not be tainted even by the appearance of a crime. He had been an honest man; his father had been an honest man; and he would rather have his brother sunk in the deepest depths of the Mississippi than that the stigma of a crime should be fastened upon him. I was awed and abashed by the dignity of his bearing and his speech.

"Buck, dare you go back to Torrentville?" he asked.

"I should only be thrown into jail if I went."

"No matter for that. Dare you trust to your own integrity for the final result?"

"I can't bring the gentleman into court to say that he gave me the money, which is the only thing against me."

"Have you told the person how you are situated, and of the charge against you?"

"No, I haven't seen him. He lives a hundred miles from Torrentville."

"I suppose so. Such witnesses are always a great way off when they are wanted," added my brother, with an ill-concealed sneer.

"I see that you think I am guilty, Clarence," I replied, wounded beyond measure at his severe conclusions.

"I confess that the affair looks to me like a trumped-up story."

"No, no, Clarence," interposed poor Flora, her eyes filled with tears, as she came to my chair and put her arm lovingly around my neck. "Dear Buckland, I know you are innocent!"

"So do I," exclaimed Emily.

"Hookie!" ejaculated Sim Gwynn, who had been sitting in silence, with his eyes and mouth wide open, but rather nervous when the battle seemed to be going against me.

I wanted to cry myself, for I felt that my brother was very hard upon me. While the others were reaching conclusions through their feelings alone, he was taking the common-sense view of the case. The facts were stubborn, as I had been obliged to acknowledge before; and all I could bring to attest my innocence was my simple word. But the conference was interrupted by the coming of the family physician, who had been sent for to see Emily. She and her father left the room.

Clarence went over the history of the robbery again; and the more he considered, the more dissatisfied he became with me. Dear Flora pleaded for a more gentle judgment, and told him how ill Ham and Mrs. Fishley treated me.

"I don't blame you for leaving the Fishleys," he added. "I blame myself for permitting you to remain there, after you complained of them; but I had just been taken into partnership with my employers, and I could not well be absent. But I do blame you for leaving them with a stain upon your character. Something must be done immediately. I will not permit them to think you are guilty, unless you are so. If you are guilty, you are no brother of mine."

"I am not guilty," I protested.

"Then you must prove it."

"I can't prove it."

"Are you willing to take your oath before God, in court, that you saw Ham Fishley take the money and burn the letter?"

"I am."

"Very well. Then you shall go to Torrentville, and face your accusers."

"I am willing to do what you think is best."

"I can't believe you are guilty of this crime; but you were foolish to run away from it."

"I will write to the person who gave me the money, and he may do as he pleases about helping me out of the scrape."

"My business is nothing compared with this matter, and I will go with you. Now, where is this raft?"

He wished to see it, and Sim and I went with him to the levee.

CHAPTER XXIV.

UP THE RIVER.

CLARENCE called a dray, and had all Flora's things conveyed to the house he was fitting up as his residence. The raft and its apparatus he sold, and he gave me the money. This was the end of the craft which had brought us on our voyage of seventeen hundred and fifty miles. We returned to the house of Mr. Goodridge in the afternoon.

The physician had only repeated his advice that Emily must have a change of climate. Her father had already decided to accompany her to the North himself. Clarence declared that Flora must not stay in the city during the sickly season. He had been married a month before, and if we had remained in Torrentville, the letter he wrote to us just before the happy event would doubtless have reached us. It had been his plan to start for New York early in August, and to return to New Orleans by the way of the West in October, taking Flora and me with him. Our unexpected arrival changed his purpose. In the course of a week it was arranged that we should go to Torrentville at once, and Mr. Goodridge and his daughter were to accompany us.

Flora and I remained at the house of the merchant during our stay in the city, though we frequently saw my brother's wife. She soon became much attached to Flora; the gentle invalid was so patient and loving that she could not help it. If there had been no cloud hanging over me, I should have been very happy in the bright prospect before me; but I hoped, when we arrived at Torrentville, that Squire Fishley would find a way to extricate me from my dilemma.

"Buck," said Clarence to me, on the day before we started, "you begin life under brighter auspices than I did. Mr. Goodridge has just paid over to me the sum of ten thousand dollars, to be invested for you, and to be paid over to you when you are of age."

"Ten thousand dollars!" I exclaimed, amazed at the magnitude of the sum.

"And the same sum for Flora. Well, twenty thousand dollars is not much for him. He is a very rich man, and Emily is his pet. He has three sons; but all of them are bad boys, and all his hope in this world rests in his daughter. You are a lucky fellow, Buck."

"I didn't think of anything of this kind," I added, filled with wonder at my good fortune.

"I don't say you didn't deserve it; for, according to all accounts, you behaved well, and the girl would certainly have been drowned if you had not saved her. I am proud of you, Buck; but I wish you were well out of this Torrentville scrape."

That worried him; and, indeed, it worried me, after I had heard so much said about it. If I had understood the matter as well in the time of it as I did afterwards, doubtless I should not have trusted to flight for safety, but faced my accusers. My sudden departure could not have failed to confirm the suspicions of Captain Fishley, and probably Ham had made the best use of the circumstances.

The next day we went on board of a fine steamer bound to St. Louis. State-rooms had been engaged for the whole party, and I should be glad to tell the story of the journey if space would permit. We enjoyed it very much, and on the way I pointed out to my companions the various objects of interest connected with the slower voyage of the raft. At first Emily was timid on board of the steamer; but her father introduced the captain to her, and he assured her that the boilers were new, and that he never raced with other boats under any circumstances. She acquired confidence. Her health had improved a great deal, and she was able to sit up all day.

At St. Louis we took another steamer, and from that were transferred to a third, which went up the Wisconsin River. When we arrived at Riverport, I felt as though I was at home, though I dreaded to appear again in Torrentville. At St. Louis I had written a long letter to Squire Fishley, narrating all the facts of the robbery of the mail, and the charge against me. I assured him I should keep the promise I had made to him, if I had to die in jail for doing so, and that he might do as he pleased about assisting me. I told him our party would be in

Riverport by the 10th of June, and wished him to write me there, advising me what to do.

On my arrival at Riverport I went to the post-office, and obtained the letter which was waiting for me. The senator wrote that he would meet me in Riverport as soon after the 10th of June as his business would permit. He thanked me very warmly for keeping his secret so well, and assured me I should not suffer for my fidelity to him.

This letter made me happy. I told Clarence that the gentleman who had given me the money was coming to my relief, and would be in Riverport within a few days. As the party were pleasantly situated at the hotel, it was decided to remain until the "mysterious personage," as Clarence called him, made his appearance. Then the awkward fact that when he did come he would be recognized, by my friends, as the tippler who had fallen overboard, would be disclosed; and I blamed myself for what I had said to them. I stated my dilemma to Clarence, and he placed the whole party under the seal of secrecy.

I had promised not to tell who had given me the money. I had not done so; but I had said enough to enable my friends to know who he was when the squire came. It was awkward, but I could not help it, though I blamed myself for saying even as much as I did.

Emily and I had become fast friends. Before we started from New Orleans, Clarence had dressed me up in a new suit of black clothes, and I flattered myself that I was not a bad-looking fellow. I was satisfied that Emily did not think I was an ill-favored young man. We had some pleasant walks at the places where we stopped.

I was very impatient for the arrival of Squire Fishley. I expected him the day after we reached Riverport; but he did not come. In the evening I went to the vicinity of the post-office, and had a view of Darky and the wagon; but it was driven by a strange boy, who had been employed to take my place. I did not care to be recognized by any one from Torrentville; but as this boy did not know me, I ventured to go up and pat my friend the black horse on the neck. The old fellow seemed to know me, and whether he enjoyed the interview or not, I am sure I did. While I was caressing the horse, the new boy came out of the office with the mail-bag in his hand. He looked curiously at me, and seemed to wonder how I happened to be on such good terms with his horse.

"What's the news up to Torrentville?" I asked.

"Nothing particular, as I know of," he replied, looking hard at me.

"Is Captain Fishley there now?"

"Yes."

"How's Ham?"

"First rate."

"How long have you driven the mail team?"

"Going on three weeks. You see the feller that drove it before robbed the mail, and had to run away."

"Did he? What became of him?"

"That's what puzzles 'em. They can't git no clew to him. He cleared about two months ago, and they hain't seen hide nor hair on him sence. Do you know him?"

"Know whom?" I asked, startled by this direct question.

"Buck Bradford, the feller that robbed the mail and run away."

"Why do you ask?"

"O, nothin'; only the postmaster here told me to tell Captain Fishley that a letter came here for Buck Bradford, and that a young feller took it out. You haven't seen nothin' on him—have you?"

I did not choose to answer this question, and I edged off, without making any reply. It appeared that I was generally known in Torrentville as the mail robber, who had run away to escape the consequences of his crime. The reflection galled me; but the day of redemption was at hand. I did not quite like it that the postmaster had sent word of my presence in Riverport to my tyrants; for I did not wish to be taken up before the arrival of my most important witness. I deemed it prudent, therefore, to keep out of sight to some extent, though I did not put myself out much about it.

Squire Fishley did not come on the second day after our arrival, to my very great disappointment, for I began to fear that I should be snapped up by some greedy constable. The keeper of the hotel, who did not recognize me in the trim suit I wore, had a very handsome keel boat, prettily painted, which he kept for the use of the pleasure travel frequenting his house. Sim and I had rowed our friends up and down the river in this boat, and I engaged it for the third day, as soon as I found that the senator was not a passenger on the down-river steamer. I intended to make a long excursion in her, as much to keep myself out of the way, as for the fun of it. I invited Emily and Flora to go, and they gladly accepted the invitation.

THE ARREST OF BUCK BRADFORD.

After breakfast we embarked, with a plentiful supply of luncheon on board, for we did not mean to return till the middle of the afternoon. I proposed to go up the creek, and then up the branch to the swamp, where we had started on our long voyage upon the raft. Sim and I pulled cheerfully, and our passengers were delighted with the trip. We entered the gloomy swamp; but the river had fallen, so that its banks were no longer covered with water. I showed Emily the place where Sim and I had built the raft. We landed, and walked up the slope far enough for her to see the house and store of the Fishleys. In the cool shade of the swamp we lunched, and enjoyed ourselves to the utmost. My fair companion was an interested listener, and wished to know every particular in regard to the raft, which had been the means of saving her life.

About three o'clock we started to return, and the passage was so pleasant that it seemed like a dream of fairy-land. I sat at the after oar, with Emily directly in front of me; and I am not altogether sure that this circumstance was not the origin of the fairy idea; at any rate, her presence enhanced the joy of the occasion. All went merry as a marriage bell till we reached a part of the river called the Ford.

At this stage of the river the water was not three feet deep; and, just as we were passing the shoalest part of the Ford, two men leaped into the water, and waded out to the boat. Sim and I were resting on our oars at the time, and so sudden was the movement that I had no time to get out of the way.

One of these men seized the boat, and the other, in whom I recognized Stevens, the constable from Torrentville, grasped me by the collar, and dragged me out of the boat to the shore.

"We have got you at last," said the officer.

"Hookie!" shouted Sim, as he stood up in the boat gazing at me, with his eyes distended, and his mouth wide open.

My tyrants had me again.

CHAPTER XXV.

TWO HOURS IN JAIL.

THE appearance of the constable was a sufficient explanation of the misfortune which had befallen me. The man with him was a stranger to me. The mail boy had delivered his message to Captain Fishley, and the constable had been sent down to Riverport to arrest me; but not finding me there, and probably learning from the hotel-keeper where I had gone, he lay in wait for me at the Ford.

The officer and his companion were unnecessarily rough and insulting to me, I thought; but when I consider the exceedingly bad reputation which I had made, I am not much surprised. I was dragged out of the boat, my legs soused into the water, and my elaborate toilet—made in view of the fact that I was to face Miss Emily Goodridge during the excursion—was badly deranged.

Of course Emily and Flora screamed when I was pulled out of the boat; but I could hardly help laughing, in spite of my mishap, when I saw Sim Gwynn standing on the seat of the boat so as to exhibit his bow legs to the best advantage, with the stupid stare of wonder and terror on his face. The boat was floating down the river with the current, bearing my companions away from me.

"Row back to the hotel, Sim, and tell my brother I have been taken up," I shouted.

"Hookie!" responded Sim.

Before I could say any more, my savage captors, with as much parade and violence as though I had been a grizzly bear, dragged me to the wagon in the road, in which sat Captain Fishley. I was satisfied that Sim, after he recovered his senses, would be able to conduct the boat in safety to the hotel, and I did not worry about my companions.

"Well, Buck Bradford," said my old tyrant, "you are caught at last."

"Yes, I am caught at last," I replied; for I had resolved to put a cheerful face upon the matter.

"What have you done with the money you stole from the letter?" he demanded, gruffly.

"I didn't steal any money from the letter. You will have to ask Ham Fishley what has become of that money."

"He seems to be dressed better than he was. I suppose he laid it out for fine clothes," added the constable.

"Do you persist in saying that Ham Fishley robbed the mail?" said the captain, angrily.

"I do; and I think I shall be able to prove it, too."

"You see, the fellow is a black-hearted scoundrel," said the postmaster, turning to the man who was a stranger to me, and who, I afterwards learned, was a post-office agent or detective. "This boy has been in my family for several years, but he tries to screen himself by laying his crime to my son."

"Have you got any money about you?" asked the constable.

"I have," I replied.

"Search him," added the captain, eagerly.

"You needn't be so savage about it," said I, when the constable came at me as though I had been a royal Bengal tiger, with dangerous claws and teeth. "I'll submit without any pounding."

I turned out my pockets. I had bought a new porte-monnaie in New Orleans, and all my funds were in it. My old one, which contained the burnt envelope, was in my carpet-bag at the hotel, so that I had no motive for concealing anything. The officer opened the porte-monnaie, and counted fifty-one dollars in bills, which he took from it. The trip down the river had cost me about seventy dollars, but the proceeds of the raft and its furniture had added twenty-five dollars to my exchequer. As my brother had paid all my expenses on the journey up the river, I had only spent a few dollars, mostly for the hotel boat.

"Here is more money than was taken from the letter," said the constable.

"That only proves that he has robbed the mail more than once," replied Captain Fishley.

The post-office agent opened his eyes, and seemed to me to look incredulous.

"Has this boy had anything to do with the mail during the last two months?" asked he.

"Not that I know of," replied the postmaster.

The agent nodded his head, and did not seem to be quite satisfied. I surmised that Ham had been robbing other letters.

"Where have you been for two months?" asked the agent, turning to me.

"I have been to New Orleans," I answered.

"You haven't been about here, then?"

"No, sir."

"Put him in the wagon, and we will drive home," said Captain Fishley.

The post-office agent took me in charge, and he was not so rude and rough as the constable. He placed me on the back seat of the wagon, and sat beside me himself. All three of my companions plied me with questions on the way, and I told them all about my trip to New Orleans on the raft.

"Is Clarence in Riverport?" asked Captain Fishley, much astonished, and I thought troubled also.

"He is."

"What did you come back here for, after you had robbed the mail?" he demanded.

"I came back to prove that I didn't rob the mail."

"I guess you can't prove that."

"I guess I can."

"How long has Clarence been in Riverport?"

"Three days."

"Why don't he come up to Torrentville and see the folks?"

"He's coming. We were waiting in Riverport to see a gentleman first," I answered.

After I had told my story, they ceased questioning me, and I had an opportunity to consider my position. Ham Fishley would not be glad to see me. It would be more convenient for him not to have any examination into the circumstances attending the robbing of the mail. From one or two remarks of the post-office agent, I had come to the conclusion that other letters than Miss Larrabee's were missing. Besides, the demeanor of this man towards me was so considerate after I told my story, that I was confident he had his doubts in regard to my guilt.

Captain Fishley drove up to the door of the store, and I was told to get out. I obeyed, and went into the store. There I saw Ham Fishley. I fancied that he looked pale, and that his lip quivered when he saw me.

"Got back—have you, Buck?" said he, with a ghastly grin.

"Yes, I've got back," I replied, with becoming dignity.

"They say the way of the transgressor is hard," he added.

"I think you will find it so, Ham, before this business is finished."

"You still lay it to me," he added, angrily.

Mrs. Fishley, hearing of my arrival, hastened into the shop to see me.

"So, you monster, you! you have come back—have you?" she began, in the same refreshing, snarling tones which had so often enlivened my existence in the past.

"I have come back, Mrs. Fishley; or rather I have been brought back," I replied, pleasantly; for I felt that I could afford to be good-natured.

"Yes, mother; and he still sticks to it that I robbed the mail—that I did!" added Ham, with the same sickly grin.

"I should like to know!" exclaimed she, placing her arms a-kimbo, and staring me full in the face. "I should like to know! Haven't we done enough for you, Buck Bradford, that you want to use us in this way? How du'st you run away, and take Flora with you? You will make her as bad as yourself byme-by."

"I hope not," I replied, smiling.

"She went all the way to New Orleans with him on a raft, and so did that Sim Gwynn," interposed the captain.

"Well, there's no end of wonders with bad boys. But where's Flora now?" asked Mrs. Fishley.

"She's at the hotel in Riverport, with Clarence and his wife."

My female tyrant wanted to know all about it, and I told her; but I will omit the torrent of snapping, snarling, and abuse she poured out upon me for my base ingratitude to her who had always treated me like a son. By this time the news had begun to circulate in the village that "the mail robber" had been caught, and men, women, and children came to see the awful monster. It was an awkward and uncomfortable situation for me; but I consoled myself by anticipating the triumphant acquittal which awaited me. When the people had gazed at me to their satisfaction, the constable conducted me to the jail. I did not shudder, as I supposed I should, when I was cast into the lonely cell, for I knew I was innocent.

I had been there but a couple of hours, when the door was opened, and Clarence came in. Sim had succeeded in navigating the boat back to the hotel, and the story of my mishap had been told by Flora.

"The steamer arrived just before I left," said my brother. "A gentleman came to the hotel inquiring for you. Who was he, Buck?"

"He will tell you himself, if he chooses. I suppose he is the person I wish to see."

"Buck, I have had my doubts from the beginning; but I feel more confident now that you are innocent," he added, taking me by the hand, and exhibiting much emotion. "I have given bail for your appearance before the magistrate in the morning, and you may come with me now."

"I just as lief stay here as not; I am innocent," I replied.

"I have been talking with the post-office detective, who appears to be a very fair man. He says a valuable letter, which failed to reach its owner, has been traced to this office since you went away. Of course you could not have taken that."

"Nor the other."

We left the jail and went to the hotel in Torrentville, where we met the detective. I gave him some information in regard to Ham Fishley's habits, and he called in the keeper of the livery stable connected with the hotel. This man assured him that Ham had paid him over thirty dollars within two months for the use of his best team. I suggested that he should visit Crofton's, and ascertain what presents Miss Elsie had received from her lover, for this was the relation my young tyrant sustained to her, in spite of his and her tender age. He was not quite willing to ask her himself, but he purposed to find out by some means. I was very sure that Ham's father had not given him thirty dollars for horse hire within two months.

I did not sleep much that night, I was so nervous and excited. Early the next morning I went down to Riverport with Clarence. As we drove by the post-office I saw Captain Fishley and the senator come out of the house. I felt safe then. How Flora hugged me when I met her! How she wept when I told her I had been put in jail! And how glad Emily was to see me!

We breakfasted with our friends, and as my examination before the magistrate was to take place at ten o'clock, the whole party started for Torrentville immediately. Sim Gwynn had some doubts about going up to Torrentville, and said "Hookie" with more than usual emphasis, when the thing was proposed to him; but Mr. Goodridge promised to save him from Barkspear's wrath, and he consented to go.

At ten o'clock our entire party, seven in number, entered the office of Squire Ward, where the preliminary examination was to take place.

CHAPTER XXVI.

CONCLUSION.

"YOU are the fellow that stole the money Ethan sent me," squealed Miss Larrabee, as I entered the office.

"Not much," I replied.

"O, but I know you did it; Ham Fishley says so, and I reckon he knows who took it."

"I reckon he does, too," I answered, as I took a seat assigned to me by the constable.

Captain Fishley and Ham soon appeared, attended by the squire, the latter of whom, to the apparent horror of his brother, took the trouble to come to me, and cordially shake my hand.

"You ought to have told me about this trouble before," said he, in a whisper.

"I meant to keep my promise, whatever happened to me," I replied, cheered by his kindness and good will.

Ham Fishley looked very pale, and his father looked very ugly. Quite a number of witnesses were present, including the postmaster of Riverport. The examination was commenced, and I pleaded not guilty. Clarence had employed the smartest lawyer in town to manage my case, and I had had a long talk with him the night before. The missing letter was traced to the Riverport office, after which it had disappeared. Captain Fishley swore that I brought the mail up to Torrentville, and Ham that he had seen me counting what appeared to be a large sum of money, on the night when the letter should have arrived, according to the testimony of the postmaster at Riverport, who distinctly remembered the address.

Then Ham was placed "on the gridiron," and slowly broiled by Squire Pollard, the lawyer who managed my case. He was asked where he spent the evening, what time he got home, when he had sorted the mail; and before he was "done," he became considerably "mixed." But Ham's time had not come yet, and he was permitted to step down.

Captain Fishley had testified that I had no means of obtaining money honestly, and that I had run away. The captain seemed to be greatly astonished when his brother was called to the witness stand for the defence.

"Mr. Fishley, were you in Torrentville two months ago?" asked Squire Pollard.

"I was," replied the senator.

"Did you see the defendant at that time?"

"Yes, sir."

"Did you give him any money?"

"Yes, sir."

"How much?"

"The young man drove me up from Riverport on the night in question. I gave him between forty and fifty dollars at that time, and enough more the next day to make a hundred dollars."

"You gave him a hundred dollars, in two payments?" repeated the lawyer, glancing round at the crowd which filled the room.

"Yes, sir, that was the amount I gave him," replied Squire Fishley; but I saw that he looked troubled.

"You gave him between forty and fifty dollars the first time?"

"Forty-six dollars, I think, was the exact amount."

"Could this have been the money which Ham Fishley saw the defendant counting in the hay-loft?"

"I have no doubt it was, as I fix the time from the testimony of the witnesses."

"Why did you pay the boy this large sum?" asked the justice.

"Because he had rendered me a very important service," answered the senator, coloring deeply.

"What was that service?" continued the magistrate.

"I had the misfortune to fall into the river, and the young man saved my life," added Squire Fishley, now very much embarrassed.

"Ah, indeed!" said the justice on the bench, nodding his head in full satisfaction.

"But the defendant refused to tell where he got the money, and the presumption was, that he stole it."

"I desired him not to mention the matter for reasons of my own."

"I submit, your honor," interposed Squire Pollard, "that this matter is foreign to the case. Squire Fishley testifies that he gave the defendant one hundred dollars, and that he desired the young man not to mention the matter. This testimony explains where the defendant obtained his money, and why he declined to tell where he got it. The material facts are all elicited."

Not only Squire Ward, but many others in the room, were very anxious to know why this silence had been imposed upon me. There was something dark about it, and the people were not satisfied. Squire Fishley was troubled, and, though my lawyer, who seemed to understand the matter,—I had told him nothing,—had influence enough to save him from any exposure, yet he was not content to leave the dark point in its present obscurity.

"There does not seem to be any good reason for this concealment," added the justice.

"All the essential facts have come out, your honor," said Squire Pollard.

"I wish to explain it fully," interposed the senator, very much to my surprise. "Since this event, I have been elected president of a total abstinence society. I took the pledge two months ago, on my return home from Torrentville."

"What has this to do with the case?" demanded the justice, impatiently.

"I will explain," resumed the senator. "I had never been in the habit of drinking more than one glass of intoxicating liquor in a day; but meeting some friends on the steamer, I exceeded my limit. In a word, I was somewhat intoxicated when I fell into the river, and this was the reason why I wished to conceal the facts. The events of that night made me a total abstinence man, and with God's help I will never taste the intoxicating cup again."

"Ah, indeed!" said the magistrate.

Squire Fishley stepped down from the stand, wiping the perspiration from his brow. After this humiliating confession, I think there was not a man present who did not respect and honor him for his manly acknowledgment.

"There appears not to be a particle of evidence against the defendant," said Squire Pollard. "I move that he be discharged."

I was discharged.

My friends gathered around me, as the court broke up, to congratulate me on the happy event. Clarence was satisfied, and how warmly Emily Goodridge pressed my trembling hand! In my heart I thanked God for this issue. Captain Fishley seemed to be stunned by the result; and Mrs. Fishley, who came in after the examination commenced, "wanted to know!" Ham was confounded; and as he was moving out of the office, the post-office agent placed a heavy hand upon his shoulder.

My junior tyrant looked ghastly pale when he was conducted back to the magistrate's table. His guilty soul was withering in his bosom. Tyrants as his father and mother had been to me, I pitied them, for they were not guilty of his crime.

"What do you mean by that?" demanded Captain Fishley, angrily, as the detective dragged his son up to the bar of justice.

"I arrest him for robbing the mail."

"Me!" exclaimed Ham, his lips as white as his face, and his knees smiting each other in his terror.

"I should like to know!" ejaculated his mother, holding up both her hands in horror and surprise.

"Do you mean to say that Ham robbed the mail!" demanded Captain Fishley.

"I am afraid he did."

"Then you are going to believe what that wretch says," gasped Mrs. Fishley, pointing to me.

The justice immediately organized his court for the examination of the new culprit, and Captain Fishley was called as the first witness.

"Does your son receive wages for his services?" asked the detective, who managed the case for the post-office.

"No, not exactly wages. I give him what money he wants."

"How much money do you give him?"

"As much as he wants," replied the witness, sourly.

"How much have you given him during the last two months?"

"I don't know."

"What do you think?"

"I don't know."

"Answer the question to the best of your knowledge and belief," interposed the justice.

"Perhaps fifteen or twenty dollars," replied the captain, determined to make the sum large enough to cover the case, though I believed that the sum he named was double the actual amount he had given Ham.

"Did it exceed twenty?"

"No, I think not."

The detective then inquired particularly into the management of the mails, as to who opened them and sorted the letters. I was then placed on the stand. I told my story, as I have related it before. I produced the fragment of the envelope I found in the fireplace on the morning after the destruction of the letter. Captain Fishley was overwhelmed, and Mrs. Fishley wrung her hands, declaring it was all "an awful lie."

Captain Fishley immediately called in Squire Pollard, who had done so well for me, to defend his son. The skilful lawyer subjected me to a severe cross-examination, in which I told the simple truth, with all the collateral circumstances about the party at Crofton's, the hour, the weather, the day, and twenty other things which he dragged in to confuse me. Truth is mighty always, in little as well as in great things, and she always stands by her friends.

The stable-keeper appeared with his memorandum-book, and astonished Captain Fishley by swearing that Ham had paid him over thirty dollars, within two months, for the use of his best team. The witness also testified that he had seen Ham pay four dollars for two suppers at the hotel in Tripleton, ten miles distant, and that the defendant had told him not to tell his father that he hired the team.

The evidence was sufficient to commit the prisoner for trial before the United States Court. His father and his uncle became his bail. The detective had also ascertained that he had given his "lady love" jewelry to the amount of at least thirty dollars, which she indignantly sent back as soon as the facts transpired.

People wanted to know why I had not told of Ham before. I had told his father, but he would not believe me. I was afraid that Squire Fishley would blame me for the testimony I had given; but he did not, much as he regretted his brother's misfortune.

Our party left the office together. As we were going out, Mr. Barkspear put his hand on Sim Gwynn's arm, and frightened him nearly out of his scanty wits. The poor fellow flew to the protection of Mr. Goodridge.

"That boy ran away from me," said the miserly farmer.

"He didn't give me enough to eat," howled Sim.

"He must go back and work for me till his time is out."

"No, sir; he shall not," interposed the wealthy merchant. "You starved him, and the obligation, if there ever was any, is cancelled."

"But I ought to have sunthin' for his time," whined Barkspear.

"Not a cent;" and Mr. Goodridge hurried Sim towards the hotel.

Sim was relieved; but Sim was not exactly a prize to any one. He was good for nothing except to work on a farm, or do the chores about the house. He was good-natured and willing. He had a hand in saving Emily Goodridge, and her father could not forget that. He found a place for him with a minister in Riverport, and left a thousand dollars in trust for his benefit.

My brother wished to go east, and I was held as a witness to appear in Ham's trial; but the culprit took to himself heels and ran away, probably by his father's advice, as the testimony against him continued to accumulate. His bail was paid, and nothing was heard of Ham for years, when I saw him tending bar on a Mississippi steamer. He was a miserable fellow. "Cutting a swell" had been his ruin, for his desire to be smart before "his girl" had tempted him to rob the mail.

I am glad to be able to say that Squire Fishley did not suffer by his honest confession of his own weakness, for he was true to his pledge, and true to his religion. He has held several high offices in this state, and will probably go to Congress in due time.

The Fishleys of Torrentville had no good will towards me, and I kept away from them. Our party remained together during the summer at the North, and in October returned to New Orleans. Flora and I went to live with Clarence, and I was employed in the store of his firm, first as a boy, then as a clerk; and when I was twenty-one, I had the capital to go into business as one of the concern.

Emily Goodridge's health was much improved by her journey to the North, and every year the same party repeated it. I need hardly say that during my clerkship I was a constant visitor at the house of Mr. Goodridge, and that his daughter and myself were the best of friends. Flora used to go there every afternoon; but she could not venture out, as I did, in the evening air.

Years rolled on, and brought their changes. I was a merchant in prosperous circumstances. Flora, in a measure, outgrew her bodily infirmities, but she was always an invalid. I heard from Sim Gwynn once in a great while. He took care of the minister's horse and his garden. He could not "keep a hotel," and he did not aspire to do so. He was contented with enough to eat and enough to wear.

I am still a young man; but our firm is Bradford Brothers. We are doing well, and in time hope to make a fortune. Whether I do so or not, I shall still be happy, for my wife—whom I picked up one day on the Mississippi River—is joy enough for this world, though I have another, and almost equal joy, in dear Flora, whose home is also mine. We are blessed of God, and blessed in ourselves, for we are as loving and devoted to each other as when, years ago, on the raft, we journeyed DOWN THE RIVER.

OLIVER OPTIC'S BOOKS

All-Over-the-World Library. By OLIVER OPTIC. First Series. Illustrated.

1. A Missing Million; OR, THE ADVENTURES OF LOUIS BELGRADE.

2. A Millionaire at Sixteen; OR, THE CRUISE OF THE "GUARDIAN MOTHER."

3. A Young Knight Errant; OR, CRUISING IN THE WEST INDIES.

4. Strange Sights Abroad; OR, ADVENTURES IN EUROPEAN WATERS.

No author has come before the public during the present generation who has achieved a larger and more deserving popularity among young people than "Oliver Optic." His stories have been very numerous, but they have been uniformly excellent in moral tone and literary quality. As indicated in the general title, it is the author's intention to conduct the readers of this entertaining series "around the world." As a means to this end, the hero of the story purchases a steamer which he names the "Guardian Mother," and with, a number of guests she proceeds on her voyage.—*Christian Work, N. Y.*

All-Over-the-World Library. By OLIVER OPTIC. Second Series. Illustrated.

1. American Boys Afloat; OR, CRUISING IN THE ORIENT.

2. The Young Navigators; OR, THE FOREIGN CRUISE OF THE "MAUD."

3. Up and Down the Nile; OR, YOUNG ADVENTURERS IN AFRICA.

4. Asiatic Breezes; OR, STUDENTS ON THE WING.

The interest in these stories is continuous, and there is a great variety of exciting incident woven into the solid information which the book imparts so generously and without the slightest suspicion of dryness. Manly boys will welcome this volume as cordially as they did its predecessors.—*Boston Gazette.*

All-Over-the-World Library. By OLIVER OPTIC. Third Series. Illustrated.

1. Across India; OR, LIVE BOYS IN THE FAR EAST.

2. Half Round the World; OR, AMONG THE UNCIVILIZED.

3. Four Young Explorers; OR, SIGHT-SEEING IN THE TROPICS.

4. Pacific Shores; OR, ADVENTURES IN EASTERN SEAS.

Amid such new and varied surroundings it would be surprising indeed if the author, with his faculty of making even the commonplace attractive, did not tell an intensely interesting story of adventure, as well as give much information in regard to the distant countries through which our friends pass, and the strange peoples with whom they are brought in contact. This book, and indeed the whole series, is admirably adapted to reading aloud in the family circle, each volume containing matter which will interest all the members of the family.—*Boston Budget.*

The Blue and the Gray—Afloat. By OLIVER OPTIC. Six volumes. Illustrated. Beautiful binding in blue and gray, with emblematic dies. Cloth. Any volume sold separately.

1. Taken by the Enemy.

2. Within the Enemy's Lines.

3. On the Blockade.

4. Stand by the Union.

5. Fighting for the Right.

6. A Victorious Union.

The Blue and the Gray—on Land.

1. Brother against Brother.

2. In the Saddle.

3. A Lieutenant at Eighteen.

4. On the Staff.

5. At the Front.

6. An Undivided Union.

"There never has been a more interesting writer in the field of juvenile literature than Mr. W. T. Adams, who, under his well-known pseudonym, is known and admired by every boy and girl in the country, and by thousands who have long since passed the boundaries of youth, yet who remember with pleasure the genial, interesting pen that did so much to interest, instruct, and entertain their younger years. 'The Blue and the Gray' is a title that is sufficiently indicative of the nature and spirit of the latest series, while the name of Oliver Optic is sufficient warrant of the absorbing style of narrative. This series is as bright and entertaining as any work that Mr. Adams has yet put forth, and will be as eagerly perused as any that has borne his name. It would not be fair to the prospective reader to deprive him of the zest which comes from the unexpected by entering into a synopsis of the story. A word, however, should be said in regard to the beauty and appropriateness of the binding, which makes it a most attractive volume."—*Boston Budget.*

Woodville Stories. By OLIVER OPTIC. Six volumes. Illustrated. Any volume sold separately.

Down the River; or, Buck Bradford and His Tyrants

1. Rich and Humble; OR, THE MISSION OF BERTHA GRANT.

2. In School and Out; OR, THE CONQUEST OF RICHARD GRANT.

3. Watch and Wait; OR, THE YOUNG FUGITIVES.

4. Work and Win; OR, NODDY NEWMAN ON A CRUISE.

5. Hope and Have; OR, FANNY GRANT AMONG THE INDIANS.

6. Haste and Waste; OR, THE YOUNG PILOT OF LAKE CHAMPLAIN.

"Though we are not so young as we once were, we relished these stories almost as much as the boys and girls for whom they were written. They were really refreshing, even to us. There is much in them which is calculated to inspire a generous, healthy ambition, and to make distasteful all reading tending to stimulate base desires." —*Fitchburg Reveille.*

The Starry Flag Series. By OLIVER OPTIC. In six volumes. Illustrated. Any volume sold separately.

1. The Starry Flag; OR, THE YOUNG FISHERMAN OF CAPE ANN.

2. Breaking Away; OR, THE FORTUNES OF A STUDENT.

3. Seek and Find; OR, THE ADVENTURES OF A SMART BOY.

4. Freaks of Fortune; OR, HALF ROUND THE WORLD.

5. Make or Break; OR, THE RICH MAN'S DAUGHTER.

6. Down the River; OR, BUCK BRADFORD AND THE TYRANTS.

"Mr. ADAMS, the celebrated and popular writer, familiarly known as OLIVER OPTIC, seems to have inexhaustible funds for weaving together the virtues of life; and, notwithstanding he has written scores of books, the same freshness and novelty run through them all. Some people think the sensational element predominates. Perhaps it does. But a book for young people needs this, and so long as good sentiments are inculcated such books ought to be read."

Army and Navy Stories. By OLIVER OPTIC. Six volumes. Illustrated. Any volume sold separately.

1. The Soldier Boy; OR, TOM SOMERS IN THE ARMY.

2. The Sailor Boy; OR, JACK SOMERS IN THE NAVY.

3. The Young Lieutenant; OR, ADVENTURES OF AN ARMY OFFICER.

4. The Yankee Middy; OR, ADVENTURES OF A NAVY OFFICER.

5. Fighting Joe; OR, THE FORTUNES OF A STAFF OFFICER.

6. Brave Old Salt; OR, LIFE ON THE QUARTER DECK.

"This series of six volumes recounts the adventures of two brothers, Tom and Jack Somers, one in the army, the other in the navy, in the great Civil War. The romantic narratives of the fortunes and exploits of the brothers are thrilling in the extreme. Historical accuracy in the recital of the great events of that period is strictly followed, and the result is, not only a library of entertaining volumes, but also the best history of the Civil War for young people ever written."

Boat Builders Series. By OLIVER OPTIC. In six volumes. Illustrated. Any volume sold separately.

1. All Adrift; OR, THE GOLDWING CLUB.

2. Snug Harbor; OR, THE CHAMPLAIN MECHANICS.

3. Square and Compasses; OR, BUILDING THE HOUSE.

4. Stem to Stern; OR, BUILDING THE BOAT.

5. All Taut; OR, RIGGING THE BOAT.

6. Ready About; OR, SAILING THE BOAT.

"The series includes in six successive volumes the whole art of boat building, boat rigging, boat managing, and practical hints to make the ownership of a boat pay. A great deal of useful information is given in this Boat Builders Series, and in each book a very interesting story is interwoven with the information. Every reader will be interested at once in Dory, the hero of 'All Adrift,' and one of the characters retained in the subsequent volumes of the series. His friends will not want to lose sight of him, and every boy who makes his acquaintance in 'All Adrift' will become his friend."

Riverdale Story Books. By OLIVER OPTIC. Twelve volumes. Illustrated. Illuminated covers. Price: cloth, per set, $3.60; per volume, 30 cents; paper, per set, $2.00.

1. Little Merchant.

2. Young Voyagers.

3. Christmas Gift.

4. Dolly and I.

5. Uncle Ben.

6. Birthday Party.

7. Proud and Lazy.

8. Careless Kate.

9. Robinson Crusoe, Jr.

10. The Picnic Party.

11. The Gold Thimble.

12. The Do-Somethings.

Riverdale Story Books. By OLIVER OPTIC. Six volumes. Illustrated. Fancy cloth and colors. Price per volume, 30 cents.

1. Little Merchant.

2. Proud and Lazy.

3. Young Voyagers.

4. Careless Kate.

5. Dolly and I.

6. Robinson Crusoe, Jr.

Flora Lee Library. By OLIVER OPTIC. Six volumes. Illustrated. Fancy cloth and colors.

1. The Picnic Party.

2. The Gold Thimble.

3. The Do-Somethings.

4. Christmas Gift.

5. Uncle Ben.

6. Birthday Party.

These are bright short stories for younger children who are unable to comprehend the Starry Flag Series or the Army and Navy Series. But they all display the author's talent for pleasing and interesting the little folks. They are all fresh and original, preaching no sermons, but inculcating good lessons.

The Great Western Series. By OLIVER OPTIC. In six volumes. Illustrated. Any volume sold separately.

1. Going West; OR, THE PERILS OF A POOR BOY.

2. Out West; OR, ROUGHING IT ON THE GREAT LAKES.

3. Lake Breezes; OR, THE CRUISE OF THE SYLVANIA.

4. Going South; OR, YACHTING ON THE ATLANTIC COAST.

5. Down South; OR, YACHT ADVENTURES IN FLORIDA.

6. Up the River; OR, YACHTING ON THE MISSISSIPPI.

"This is the latest series of books issued by this popular writer, and deals with life on the Great Lakes, for which a careful study was made by the author in a summer tour of the immense water sources of America. The story, which carries the same hero through the six books of the series, is always entertaining, novel scenes and varied incidents giving a constantly changing yet always attractive aspect to the narrative. OLIVER OPTIC has written nothing better."

The Yacht Club Series. By OLIVER OPTIC. In six volumes. Illustrated. Any volume sold separately.

1. Little Bobtail; OR, THE WRECK OF THE PENOBSCOT.

2. The Yacht Club; OR, THE YOUNG BOAT BUILDERS.

3. Money-Maker; OR, THE VICTORY OF THE BASILISK.

4. The Coming Wave; OR, THE TREASURE OF HIGH ROCK.

5. The Dorcas Club; OR, OUR GIRLS AFLOAT.

6. Ocean Born; OR, THE CRUISE OF THE CLUBS.

"The series has this peculiarity, that all of its constituent volumes are independent of one another, and therefore each story is complete in itself. OLIVER OPTIC is, perhaps, the favorite author of the boys and girls of this country, and he seems destined to enjoy an endless popularity. He deserves his success, for he makes very interesting stories, and inculcates none but the best sentiments, and the 'Yacht Club' is no exception to this rule."—*New Haven Journal and Courier.*

Onward and Upward Series. By OLIVER OPTIC. In six volumes. Illustrated. Any volume sold separately.

1. Field and Forest; OR, THE FORTUNES OF A FARMER.

2. Plane and Plank; OR, THE MISHAPS OF A MECHANIC.

3. Desk and Debit; OR, THE CATASTROPHES OF A CLERK.

4. Cringle and Crosstree; OR, THE SEA SWASHES OF A SAILOR.

5. Bivouac and Battle; OR, THE STRUGGLES OF A SOLDIER.

6. Sea and Shore; OR, THE TRAMPS OF A TRAVELLER.

"Paul Farringford, the hero of these tales, is, like most of this author's heroes, a young man of high spirit, and of high aims and correct principles, appearing in the different volumes as a farmer, a captain, a bookkeeper, a soldier, a sailor, and a traveller. In all of them the hero meets with very exciting adventures, told in the graphic style for which the author is famous."

The Lake Shore Series. By OLIVER OPTIC. In six volumes. Illustrated. Any volume sold separately.

1. Through by Daylight; OR, THE YOUNG ENGINEER OF THE LAKE SHORE RAILROAD.

2. Lightning Express; OR, THE RIVAL ACADEMIES.

3. On Time; OR, THE YOUNG CAPTAIN OF THE UCAYGA STEAMER.

4. Switch Off; OR, THE WAR OF THE STUDENTS.

5. Brake Up; OR, THE YOUNG PEACEMAKERS.

6. Bear and Forbear; OR, THE YOUNG SKIPPER OF LAKE UCAYGA.

"OLIVER OPTIC is one of the most fascinating writers for youth, and withal one of the best to be found in this or any past age. Troops of young people hang over his vivid pages; and not one of them ever learned to be mean, ignoble, cowardly, selfish, or to yield to any vice from anything they ever read from his pen." —*Providence Press.*

The Famous Boat Club Series. By OLIVER OPTIC. Six volumes. Illustrated. Any volume sold separately.

1. The Boat Club; OR, THE BUNKERS OF RIPPLETON.

2. All Aboard; OR, LIFE ON THE LAKE.

3. Now or Never; OR, THE ADVENTURES OF BOBBY BRIGHT.

4. Try Again; OR, THE TRIALS AND TRIUMPHS OF HARRY WEST.

5. Poor and Proud; OR, THE FORTUNES OF KATY REDBURN.

6. Little by Little; OR, THE CRUISE OF THE FLYAWAY.

"This is the first series of books written for the young by OLIVER OPTIC. It laid the foundation for his fame as the first of authors in which the young delight, and gained for him the title of the Prince of Story Tellers. The six books are varied in incident and plot, but all are entertaining and original."

(*Other volumes in preparation.*)

Young America Abroad: A LIBRARY OF TRAVEL AND ADVENTURE IN FOREIGN LANDS. By OLIVER OPTIC. Illustrated by NAST and others. First Series. Six volumes. Any volume sold separately.

1. Outward Bound; OR, YOUNG AMERICA AFLOAT.

2. Shamrock and Thistle; OR, YOUNG AMERICA IN IRELAND AND SCOTLAND.

3. Red Cross; OR, YOUNG AMERICA IN ENGLAND AND WALES.

4. Dikes and Ditches; OR, YOUNG AMERICA IN HOLLAND AND BELGIUM.

5. Palace and Cottage; OR, YOUNG AMERICA IN FRANCE AND SWITZERLAND.

6. Down the Rhine; OR, YOUNG AMERICA IN GERMANY.

"The story from its inception, and through the twelve volumes (see Second Series), is a bewitching one, while the information imparted concerning the countries of Europe and the isles of the sea is not only correct in every particular, but is told in a captivating style. OLIVER OPTIC will continue to be the boys' friend, and his pleasant books will continue to be read by thousands of American boys. What a fine holiday present either or both series of 'Young America Abroad' would be for a young friend! It would make a little library highly prized by the recipient, and would not be an expensive one."—*Providence Press.*

Young America Abroad. By OLIVER OPTIC. Second Series. Six volumes. Illustrated. Any volume sold separately.

1. Up the Baltic; OR, YOUNG AMERICA IN NORWAY, SWEDEN, AND DENMARK.

2. Northern Lands; OR, YOUNG AMERICA IN RUSSIA AND PRUSSIA.

3. Cross and Crescent; OR, YOUNG AMERICA IN TURKEY AND GREECE.

4. Sunny Shores; OR, YOUNG AMERICA IN ITALY AND AUSTRIA.

5. Vine and Olive; OR, YOUNG AMERICA IN SPAIN AND PORTUGAL.

6. Isles of the Sea; OR, YOUNG AMERICA HOMEWARD BOUND.

"OLIVER OPTIC is a *nom de plume* that is known and loved by almost every boy of intelligence in the land. We have seen a highly intellectual and world-weary man, a cynic whose heart was somewhat embittered by its large experience of human nature, take up one of OLIVER OPTIC'S books, and read it at a sitting, neglecting his work in yielding to the fascination of the pages. When a mature and exceedingly well-informed mind, long despoiled of all its freshness, can thus find pleasure in a book for boys, no additional words of recommendation are needed."—*Sunday Times.*

Lightning Source UK Ltd.
Milton Keynes UK
UKHW040916270620
365672UK00002B/235